MALLORY'S CHRISTMAS WISH

**Other books by
Ann M. Martin**

Rachel Parker, Kindergarten Show-off
Eleven Kids, One Summer
Ma and Pa Dracula
Yours Turly, Shirley
Ten Kids, No Pets
Slam Book
Just a Summer Romance
Missing Since Monday
With You and Without You
Me and Katie (the Pest)
Stage Fright
Inside Out
Bummer Summer

BABY-SITTERS LITTLE SISTER series
THE BABY-SITTERS CLUB mysteries
THE BABY-SITTERS CLUB series
(see back of book for a complete listing)

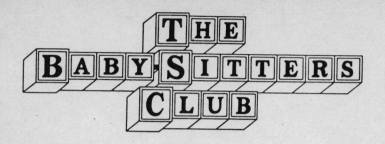

MALLORY'S CHRISTMAS WISH

Ann M. Martin

AN
APPLE
PAPERBACK

SCHOLASTIC INC.
New York Toronto London Auckland Sydney

Cover art by Hodges Soileau

ISBN 0-590-22876-6

12 11 10 9 8 7 6 5   3 4 5 6 7 8 9/0

Printed in the U.S.A.   40

First Scholastic printing, December 1995

*The author gratefully acknowledges
Peter Lerangis
for his help in
preparing this manuscript.*

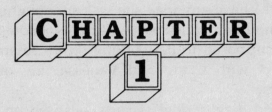

CHAPTER 1

It was a cold, snowy night. There was a white circle on the windowpane from the frost. It was the day after Thanksgiving. Inside the old, crumbling house of the Post family, a fire burned. Shivering from the frigidity, the heat was not enough for the seven Post children huddled around.

Little did they know that outside in the darkness, a pair of eyes was looking in.

"Mallory, what's friddiggity?" asked my sister Margo.

"Huh?" I said with a start.

Did I have any idea she was snooping over my shoulder while I was writing? Nooooo. She was supposed to be working on a Christmas project with Claire and Vanessa, my other sisters.

"Frid diggity dog!" Claire collapsed on the living room floor, giggling.

That made my brothers Nicky and Jordan race into the room. "What's so funny?" asked Nicky.

"I thought you were cutting out snowflakes," I scolded Margo, "not spying."

Jordan rolled his eyes. "Did she need to ask permission, Your Highness?"

"Sorry, Mallory," Margo said sheepishly.

"Dig miggidy mog!" Claire squealed.

"I said, what's so funny?" demanded Nicky.

"Your face," called my brother Adam from the kitchen.

He and Byron (yes, another brother) howled with laughter.

"Okay, guys, dinnertime!" called my dad.

"Daaaaaaad, they're teasing me again!" Nicky whined, running into the kitchen.

I closed my spiral notebook and stood up. Near the fireplace, Vanessa was busy writing

2

poetry in a composition book. "Come on, Vanessa," I urged her.

"In a minute," she said. "I'm thinking of a rhyme for 'reindeer.' "

I followed Margo into the kitchen. "I want some friddiggity for dessert." she announced.

"What's friddiggity?" Mom asked.

"Dog diggity fridge," Claire replied.

Dad spun around. "The dog's in the fridge?"

As Byron fell off his chair in hysterics, Adam yanked open the refrigerator and gasped. "Pow's frozen solid!"

Poor Claire turned bone-white.

Do you live in a monkey house? I do. My life story will be called *Mallory and the Seven Simian Siblings*. (Isn't *simian* a great word? It means "of or relating to monkeys.")

I, Mallory Pike, am Eldest Monkey. I'm eleven and I'm in sixth grade. Maybe you've figured out that I want to be a professional writer someday. (Don't judge the story I was writing, though. That was just a first draft.) On the day you see me accepting a Newbery medal, I will have clear blue eyes and perfect teeth. And maybe my red hair will be less unruly. Now, however, I wear braces and glasses. And my hair is a sight. Contacts would change my life, but my parents believe I am a baby and refuse to let me have them.

"Out of the question until you're fifteen," says my father.

Of course, Mom and Dad aren't nearly as strict with my brothers and sisters. That is the worst part about being Eldest Monkey. Honestly, by the time Claire is eleven, she'll have an apartment of her own, a personal butler, and a salary.

Claire, by the way, is five. Margo's seven, Nicky's eight, and Vanessa's nine. Adam, Jordan, and Byron are ten-year-old triplets.

The triplets were snickering at Claire. She was looking through the back door, making sure our dog, Pow, was still alive and in his house. Margo and I reached into a drawer by the stove to pull out our usual load of silverware (Dad calls it "the armament").

Nicky was sniffing loudly. "What stinks?"

"Are you referring to my gourmet lamb stew?" Dad said, stirring a big pot on the stove.

"Lamb stew?" Byron looked horrified.

Vanessa strolled into the kitchen, reciting, "Lamb stew, lamb stew. Start with some herbs, then chop up the ewe."

"That's disgusting," I said.

"What's a ewe?" Claire asked.

"A female lamb," Vanessa replied.

"Ewwwww!" Margo cried.

Vanessa grinned. "Exactly."

"Who ever heard of Christmas lamb stew?" Jordan protested. "We're supposed to do Christmasy stuff, remember?"

Mom raised an eyebrow. "What, exactly, do you consider a Christmasy dinner?"

"Turkey," Jordan replied.

"Goose," Margo said.

Adam honked.

"Gingerbread men," Claire suggested.

"*People*," I corrected her.

"People?" Claire burst out laughing. "Silly, we're not canimals."

"I meant *gingerbread* people," I said. "Not just gingerbread men. And it's *cannibals*."

Mom was looking at us as if we'd lost our minds. "What are you talking about?"

"We could make figgy pudding," Vanessa piped up.

"*Whaaaat?*" Nicky said.

"You know, like the song." Vanessa began singing to the tune of "We Wish You a Merry Christmas": "Oh, bring us some figgy pudding, oh, bring us some figgy pudding . . ."

I told you our house is crazy.

Okay, I have to admit, part of it was my fault. I had dreamed up a master plan for the Christmas season, and everyone was contributing to it.

The idea had hit me the day before, which also happened to be the day after Thanksgiving. At the time, I was Jezebel Cassoulet. My best friend, Jessica Ramsey (called Jessi), was my sister, Daphne. We were French refugees, visiting London for the first time.

Actually we were walking down Main Street of Stoneybrook, Connecticut (that's where we live). The stores had already installed their holiday window displays, a snow flurry was falling, and a Santa on the corner was ringing a bell for a charity. The street looked like a quaint village in nineteenth-century England, if you squinted and tried to ignore the neon signs, electrical wires, and cars.

Daphne and I linked arms to protect each other against the rough climate and the gruff people with their odd accents. Perhaps we would find a kind stranger who would welcome us with the hospitality and cheer of the season —

"Preholiday countdown!" a voice blared over a loudspeaker. *"Open a charge account and receive a free gift while supplies last. For all your holiday needs, Whatley's is the spirit of shopping. Remember, Christmas and Hanukkah are us!"*

My eyes unsquinted. After the voice stopped, the loudspeaker began playing a tinny version of "Jingle Bell Rock." Two kids skateboarded around us, yelling, "Yo, heads up!" A car horn rang out in the street as someone made a sudden U-turn. Outside Whatley's, a little boy was throwing a tantrum, shooting his mom with a plastic gun.

So much for nineteenth-century England.

Jessi and I looked in the window of Whatley's. A Santa mannequin was trimming a white plastic tree that blinked WHATLEY'S in purple neon script. Beside him were a dirty bag of coal labeled NAUGHTY and a huge Whatley's gift bag labeled NICE.

"How corny," Jessi remarked.

"How stupid," I said.

But we both kept staring at the display. "Have you started shopping yet?" Jessi asked.

"No. You?"

"No."

A sign in the corner of the display read ONLY FOUR MORE SHOPPING WEEKS. I began to worry. Do you know what it's like to shop for nine family members? Keeping track of what they want is impossible. Was Nicky too old for action figures? Which video games did the triplets already have? What was the book Vanessa had told me she wanted?

Suddenly the holiday season felt about as much fun as a math exam.

I was supposed to feel happy. I was supposed to be filled with the spirit of giving.

Which was different from the "spirit of shopping," whatever *that* meant.

That was when I had my idea. It went off in my head like fireworks.

This year, the Pike family would have an old-style Christmas season. Nothing would be commercial, nothing artificial. We'd make our own gifts. We could even make our cards and wrapping paper. We'd cook special holiday meals and keep the fireplace stocked with wood. Our tree would be real (of course), strung with cranberries and popcorn and homemade ornaments.

I had shivers just thinking about it.

At a family meeting that night, I brought up the idea. The reaction?

"YEEEEEEEEEEAAAHH!"

Well, something like that. From my siblings, that is. My mom and dad smiled and gave each other a "we'll discuss this" look.

The next day they agreed, and Operation Old-fashioned Christmas began.

Which brings me back to the Saturday of the lamb stew. My mom and dad patiently explained to Nicky that we had about ninety meals to prepare before Christmas, and not all of them could be strictly Christmasy.

"At least you could give us something green and red," Nicky said with a pout.

"We could dye the mashed potatoes," Dad suggested.

Mom said no. As a compromise, she served mint jelly and cranberry sauce.

You can imagine what a typical dinner with my family is like. Total chaos. That night's dinner was no exception. No one could stop talking about the holiday plan.

"I think we should hire Bert to clean the chimney for Santa," Claire said.

"Who's Bert?" Adam asked.

Claire rolled her eyes. "The guy in *Mary Poppins*, silly."

"We have to do everything super old-fashioned," Vanessa said. "Candles instead of lights . . ."

"A horse and carriage instead of our car," Margo added.

"A laser light show on the lawn," Nicky suggested.

Dad laughed. "Just like the olden days."

"I know," I said. "We could have a big open house on Christmas Day, for the whole neighborhood."

"No!" Mom blurted out. "I mean, usually people drop by informally on Christmas Eve anyway. Wouldn't it be more old-fashioned and cozy to have a nice, quiet family day on Christmas?"

Right away I thought of my dad's uncle, who lives in an elder care home called Stoneybrook Manor. "Can we invite Uncle Joe?" I asked. "He's part of the family."

Mom and Dad gave each other a Look. Uncle Joe is not the easiest person to have around. For one thing, he's in the early stages of Alzheimer's disease, and sometimes he says things that make no sense. He can be cranky, too, and he hates to leave his room. But underneath it all, he's really sweet. And he has visited our house before, so maybe he wouldn't put up a fuss.

"I'll call him," Dad said with a shrug. "But don't count on him saying yes. You know how he is."

After dinner, we scattered to continue our projects. The triplets were collecting old vinyl Christmas records and recording their favorite songs onto a tape in the rec room. Margo gave up her snowflake cutting and disappeared into her bedroom with Mom and some knitting supplies. Nicky announced he needed privacy, then clomped down to the basement and started hammering away in Dad's workshop.

As Vanessa and I returned to the living room to continue writing, I could see Claire dancing in the rec room to Elvis Presley's version of "White Christmas."

Reading over my story, I decided it was awful. "Inside the old, crumbling house of the Post family, a fire burned"? That sounded as if the house were on fire.

I changed it.

"Shivering from the frigidity, the heat was not enough for the seven Post children huddled around"? Well, "frigidity" had to go, after the way everyone made fun of it. Not to mention that I'd made it sound as if the *heat* were shivering. Also, I hadn't said exactly *what* the children had huddled around.

I changed all of that, too.

When I read ". . . outside in the darkness, a pair of eyes was looking in," I pictured two eyeballs floating around in the snow.

Writing's fun, but boy, you have to watch yourself.

As I was rewriting, Vanessa slapped down her pencil and said, "I have it! Listen: 'Santa Claus put on his coat and bandaged up his sprained ear; then he jumped into his sled and called out to his reindeer.' "

"Sprained ear?" I asked.

"From listening to too many squeaky little elf voices," Vanessa explained.

"Oh."

Dad poked his head into the room. "Mallory?" he said. "I just talked to Uncle Joe. He was full of excuses. Something about a fund-raiser at the Manor. They want to build

11

a new wing, so the residents are putting together a big holiday boutique, selling donated stuff — "

"And Uncle Joe is involved?" I was shocked. Knowing Uncle Joe, he'd want to be as far away from a big crowd scene as possible.

Dad laughed. "No. He's nervous about it, though. Thinks there'll be too many strangers wandering around, making noise. So he wants to hibernate and see no one until it's long over. Problem is, it lasts five days. I told him we were just having a family gathering, nobody else. Nice, peaceful, all of us on our best behavior. I think that's what made him agree."

"All riiight!" I said.

"Yyyyyyes!" Vanessa cried out.

Boy, did I feel great. Christmas was falling into place.

Christmas the way it should be.

CHAPTER 2

"A tizzy?" Jessi asked. "What's a tizzy?"

"Ishashoka," answered Claudia Kishi, with a mouthful of Milk Duds.

"Swallow, please," said Stacey McGill.

"I don't know her," mumbled Abigail Stevenson, grimacing at Claudia.

Claudia gulped down her Duds. "It's a kind of old car."

"That's Tin Lizzie," Kristy Thomas corrected her.

"Tizzy could be a contraption," Abby suggested.

"Con*trac*tion," Stacey McGill said.

"Exactly," Abby shot back. "Just testing you."

Mary Anne Spier giggled. "This sounds like a quiz show."

I already mentioned that Jessi's my best friend. What I didn't tell you was that I have five other close friends. We're all members of a group called the Baby-sitters Club.

We had just started our Monday meeting in official BSC headquarters, Claudia's bedroom. We also meet on Wednesdays and Fridays, from five-thirty to six on all three days. During that time we take phone calls from local parents who need baby-sitters. But between calls, it's like one big pajama party. We have the best time.

We were in an especially goofy mood that day. Why? One word: snow. December had just begun, but we were already having another flurry. (I *love* snow.)

During the meeting, I mentioned my Christmas idea. I told everyone I'd talked to Uncle Joe on Sunday, and he'd said that all the Stoneybrook Manor residents were "in a tizzy" about their upcoming fund-raiser (which was officially called the Stoneybrook Manor Christmas Boutique).

I tried to think of another word for tizzy. "It's like being in a dither," I offered.

Six blank faces.

"Isn't that some kind of musical instrument?" Abby asked.

(It's not. A *zither* is. I found that out later from Abby's twin sister, Anna, who's a good musician.)

"It means going crazy," I explained. "Being excited. The residents have formed all these

14

committees — phone canvassing, advertising, interior design, mailing list, inventory. Uncle Joe says they're running around like thirty-year-olds."

Claudia looked confused. "Is that supposed to be young?"

"To him," I replied.

"They ought to hire Kristy to help out," Jessi remarked.

"They'd all have heart attacks," Stacey said.

Kristy raised an eyebrow. "For your information, I am very gentle and lovable with old people."

"It's just the young ones she drives crazy," Abby said with a smile.

"Ahem." Kristy cleared her throat. "Perhaps we should review our policy regarding new members."

"Yikes," squeaked Abby (who happens to be our newest member). "I'll behave."

"Time for a little sweetness in the room." Claudia reached between the boards of her easel and pulled out a hidden bag of Heath bars.

As she passed them around, Kristy barged on. "I think it would be fun to help with this boutique."

"Uh-oh," Jessi said under her breath. "I smell an Idea."

"We could contribute tons of stuff," Kristy

continued. "Art, cookies, clothes. Claud, you could do a painting or sculpture or something."

"How did I know she'd say that?" Claudia asked.

Kristy was on a roll. "We could organize the kids we sit for into groups to bake bread and cookies. Mary Anne, maybe you could put together a knitting project. . . ."

We sat back and listened. That's all you can do when Kristy has one of her Ideas. Hear her out and then tell her she's crazy or brilliant.

Kristy has Ideas the way other eighth-graders have pimples: in bunches. Unlike pimples, though, most of her ideas are pretty terrific. That's why we listen, even when she's being a pain.

You know what Kristy's number one best Idea was? The Baby-sitters Club! Yup, she invented it, all by herself. She also invented Kid-Kits, which are boxes full of toys, games, and books we take with us to sitting jobs. And Kristy's Krushers, a softball team for kids who are athletically challenged. And just about every holiday event and advertising scheme the BSC has ever had.

Basically the BSC is a simple concept: a group of excellent sitters parents can reach at one central number. Making the concept work is not so simple. For example, where do you meet? What phone do you use? How do parents find out about you? When are they supposed to call? How do you coordinate jobs among members?

Kristy solved all of that. She made sure the club was set up like a super-efficient company. We have regular meeting times, officers, an official record book, and our own phone number (Claudia's private line). We even keep a notebook in which we write about our jobs. That's so all members can be kept up-to-date on our charges — their latest likes, dislikes, and special problems.

Of course, Kristy's the BSC president. She runs the meetings with an iron fist. Forget about being late. For someone so short, Kristy can be intimidating.

How short is she? Shorter than me (she's five feet even and I'm five one). I like that. You see, it's bad enough that Jessi and I are two years younger than the other members. It's even worse that our parents don't allow us to baby-sit late on weeknights. And neither of us is crazy about being called (barf, gag) "junior members." So being taller than Kristy is kind of nice.

I will never, however, be richer than Kristy, unless I win the lottery. Her stepdad, Watson Brewer, is a millionaire, and her family lives in a mansion. You'd never know all that by looking at Kristy. She lets her dark brown hair hang plainly, never wears makeup, and always dresses super-casually. Actually, Kristy wasn't born wealthy. She was in seventh grade when her mom married Watson. Before then, the Thomases lived across the street from Claudia. Mr. Thomas abandoned the family when Kristy was six, leaving Kristy, her mom, and three brothers (Charlie, Sam, and David Michael, who are now seventeen, fifteen, and seven).

Now things are happier but still crowded. Kristy's family includes Emily Michelle, a two-year-old Vietnamese girl the Brewers adopted; Nannie, Kristy's grandmother, who moved in to help care for Emily Michelle; Karen and Andrew, Watson's two children from his previous marriage, who live in the house during alternate months; a puppy; a cat; two goldfish; and a crab and a rat that travel with Karen and Andrew.

At our meeting, Kristy went on for a few minutes about the Christmas Boutique, then asked for any more business.

"Dues day!" Stacey called out.

We all grumbled and reached for our money. Claudia dug into her pants pocket and pulled out two large, melted chocolate coins.

"Oops. So that's where I put those."

Riiiing!

Without thinking, Claudia picked up the receiver with her chocolate-stained hand. "Babysitters Club! . . . Oh, hi, Mrs. Kuhn. . . ."

Kuhn sounded more like *Keewwwwn*. Claudia was staring in horror at the melted chocolate she'd smeared on the receiver.

We tried hard not to crack up.

Claudia is the BSC vice-president (mainly because we use her room and phone). She is also the world's biggest junk-food fan. Her idea of grains, protein, vegetable, and fruit? Potato chips, a Chunkie, carrot cake, and a banana split. No one knows how she stays thin. She claims it's because of the "Kishi Scientific Ener-joy Theory": if you eat what you like, you become happy, and the energy from your joy burns off calories.

Most of the time, fortunately, Claudia stays away from science. Art is her strong point. She's a great painter, sculptor, illustrator, and jewelry maker. And she puts together the coolest, most original outfits from stuff she finds in thrift stores.

Claudia is second-generation Japanese-American. That means her grandparents were immigrants. Her grandmother Mimi lived with the Kishis until she died. Mimi was Claudia's soulmate. She understood Claudia more deeply than anyone else in her family. Mr. and Mrs. Kishi are very strict. If they knew

Claudia hid junk food in her room, they'd freak. (Claudia also hides Nancy Drew books, because her parents believe she should read only the classics.) They love Claudia and appreciate her artistic side (kind of), but you can tell they have a better understanding of her sister, Janine, who's a real genius.

The closest the BSC has to a genius is Stacey McGill. She's a math whiz, which is why she is club treasurer. She collects dues, keeps track of the money, and pays our expenses (Claudia's phone bill; gas money for Charlie Thomas, who drives Kristy and Abby to meetings; stuff for Kid-Kits; and so on).

Stacey is blonde and sophisticated. Her clothes are cool in a different way than Claudia's — chic and sophisticated instead of funky and fun. Stacey grew up in New York City, which makes her one of the BSC's three transplants. (She hates that term. It makes her sound like she's a kidney or something.) She first moved to Stoneybrook when her dad's company transferred him here. Just as they were settling in, the company switched him *back* to NYC. Then her parents, who hadn't been getting along very well, divorced. When Mrs. McGill moved back to Stoneybrook, Stacey went with her.

Stoneybrook is a short train ride from the

Big Apple, so Stacey still visits her dad pretty often. In a way, she has the best of both worlds. But being a divorced kid makes her sad sometimes. She feels pulled apart, trying to please both parents.

Stacey has one other major difficulty to cope with: diabetes. Her body can't regulate the level of sugar in her blood. She needs to have meals on a strict schedule, and she can't eat refined sugars (Claudia always makes sure to have pretzels or chips on hand for her). Stacey also has to inject herself daily with a drug called insulin. (Yes, inject. Stacey insists it's not as disgusting as it sounds.)

Sometimes Stacey feels self-conscious about her diabetes, especially around guys. She used to think people would be grossed out if they knew about it. Her current boyfriend, Robert, doesn't feel that way at all. He's so considerate. He knows her eating schedule to the minute, and he never makes her feel awkward.

Stacey's not the only BSC member to have a boyfriend. So do Mary Anne, Kristy, and I. Well, Mary Anne definitely does. Kristy's boyfriend, Bart Taylor, is kind of a sports rival/pal/sometimes date. He coaches the team that plays Kristy's Krushers. Me? I go out with a guy named Ben Hobart to school dances and stuff. We don't actually call each other boyfriend and girlfriend, but we don't *not*, either, if you know what I mean.

Mary Anne and Logan Bruno have been together forever. At least it seems that way. He's another transplant, from Louisville, Kentucky. He also happens to be an associate member of the BSC, which means he baby-sits when he can (if we're extra busy), but doesn't have to attend meetings or pay dues.

You should see Mary Anne when Logan does come to meetings. She blushes the whole time. She's the shyest person I know. Also the kindest and most sensitive. And teariest. If you invite her to your house to watch a sad movie, you'd better provide lots of tissues. Either that or plastic slipcovers for your couch.

Mary Anne's personality is about the opposite of Kristy's, but the two of them are all-time best friends. As Stacey would say, "Go figure." Actually, they did grow up next door to each other. And they look sort of alike. Mary Anne's a little over five feet tall and has dark brown hair, but it's shorter than Kristy's. They also went through a lot together. Like Kristy, Mary Anne was raised by a single parent. Mrs. Spier died when Mary Anne was still a baby. Her dad was absolutely destroyed by that. For years afterward, he was strict and overprotective and nervous. By seventh grade

Mary Anne still had to dress like a little girl and go to bed unbelievably early. Mr. Spier did begin to loosen up, though, especially after he remarried the divorced mom of a former BSC member, Dawn Schafer. (Dawn has moved back to California, and boy, does Mary Anne miss her.) Now Mary Anne and her family live in the coolest two-hundred-year-old farmhouse, which is haunted by the ghost of a former owner. (True.)

Patience is another of Mary Anne's great qualities. Incredible patience. As BSC secretary, she has to oversee the club record book, which includes a master calendar and a client list. On the calendar she schedules all our jobs, making sure they don't conflict with our doctor and dentist appointments, after-school activities, and family trips. When a call comes in, she has to know who's available, and she tries to distribute jobs equally. And she's constantly updating the client list with names and phone numbers and rates paid, plus the latest information about our charges.

You know what Abby once said? "If the BSC were a car, Kristy would be the headlights, Claudia would be the chassis, Stacey would be the gas gauge, and Mary Anne would be the engine." (When Kristy asked, "What would you be?" Abby replied, "The bumper.")

That's Abby. We're still getting used to her

sense of humor. As I said, she's our newest member. She took over Dawn's job, alternate officer. That means she fills in for any officer who might be absent from a meeting.

Abby's another transplant. She moved here from Long Island with her mom and twin sister, Anna. Her dad died in a car accident when she was nine. (None of us has been brave enough to talk to her much about that.)

In some ways, Abby is like Kristy. She's outgoing and athletic, and she tends to speak before she thinks. But she's more easygoing and less competitive than Kristy and already has loads of friends in school. She also has the most gorgeous long, dark, curly hair. Kristy and Abby get along okay, but Kristy can be really crabby with her. (Don't ever tell Kristy I said this, but I think she's a little jealous of Abby.)

In another way, Abby is like Stacey. She also has a lifelong health problem. Hers is asthma, and she always carries an inhaler with her in case she has an attack. She also has allergies to dust, pollen, and certain foods.

When the Stevenson twins moved to Stoneybrook, we asked them both to be BSC members. Unfortunately, Anna said no. She's a gifted musician, and she felt regular baby-sitting would cut into her practicing time. (Which is too bad; we all really love Anna.)

Who are the most important BSC members? Why, Jessi and me, of course! Well, we're definitely the unsung heroes. We may be junior members, but we sure do our share of sitting, especially during the weekends and daytime hours.

Jessi is my best friend ever. We're very alike (except in terms of looks — she's black and I'm white). Both of us love to read, especially horse stories. We've read everything ever written by Marguerite Henry and all the *Black Beauty* books, and we know exactly when the newest *Saddle Club* book will arrive in the bookstores. Jessi's also the oldest kid in her family, so of course her parents treat her like a baby, too. She has an eight-year-old sister named Becca and a one-and-a-half-year-old brother named John Philip (Squirt, for short).

Oh, one major difference between us: Jessi's a phenomenal ballerina who takes regular dance lessons and performs in recitals and shows. I'm your basic klutz.

Jessi's family used to live in a racially mixed community in Oakley, New Jersey. When they moved to Stoneybrook, which is mostly white, they had to face some really stupid and insulting attitudes. I'm happy to say things have become easier for the Ramseys since then, but it sure was painful for them to go through it.

Okay, back to our Monday meeting. The

phone kept ringing, and by five-fifty we had booked four jobs. Claudia had managed to wipe the chocolate off the phone, and now she was passing around mini Mars bars.

After the last call, Kristy had that *I'm thinking of something* look in her eye again. "I move we discuss holiday festivities!" she announced.

Stacey groaned. "We already said we'd call the Manor, Kristy."

"Not that," Kristy replied. "What about a party for us? Wouldn't that be fun? We can make it an everything celebration — Christmas, Hanukkah, Kwanzaa — "

Claudia nearly choked on her Mars bar. "Great!" she managed to cough out.

Everyone began speaking at once. I loved the idea. A cozy family Christmas and a BSC holiday party? What could be better? This was going to be the warmest, happiest December ever. I just knew it.

CHAPTER 3

"On the twelfth day of Christmas, my true love gave to me . . ." Mom sang out.

She pointed the little cassette recorder to Nicky.

"Twelve, um . . . velociraptor eggs!" He beamed. "You know, like a dozen? And then, when you crack them, *Raaaaawr!*"

"The tape's running," Vanessa muttered.

Together, we sang the rest of the song we'd just improvised: "Eleven socks a-stinking, ten bags of Snickers, nine leaping wombats, eight soggy tacos, seven bologna-and-peanut-butter sandwiches, six silly-billy-goo-goos, fiiiiive hornet stiiiiings . . . four crawling nerds, three stooges, two curdled gloves, and some garbage in a bare tree!"

Mom clicked off the recorder. Margo and I fell back into the couch pillows, laughing. The triplets exchanged high, low, and every other imaginable kind of fives. Claire, Nicky, and

Vanessa collapsed into giggles on the floor.

"Play it back," Byron yelled.

My mom had already pressed the rewind button. When the tape reached the beginning she played it:

"On the first day of Christmas . . ." our voices began.

Ding-dong.

"I'll get it!" three or four of my siblings shouted.

Mom turned off the recorder. "I knew it. It's the Christmas Carol Police, coming to arrest us."

"Really?" Claire said, bolting to her feet.

"Just kidding, sweetheart," Mom reassured her.

She stood up and walked to the door, just as Jordan yanked it open.

A man stood on the porch. The first thing I noticed about him was his tan. You don't see too many tanned people in Stoneybrook at this time of year. The second thing I noticed was his smile, huge and warm and comfortable, as if he knew us.

"Mrs. Pike?" he said.

"Yes," my mom answered.

"Is it the policeman?" Claire asked shakily.

The man laughed loudly. "No! Oh, indeed, no. My name is Chad Henry. I'm a producer/director for Channel Three TV, and I wanted to congratulate you in person. You've been selected out of hundreds of contestants — "

Vanessa came running to the door. She looked about ready to levitate. "The Old-fashioned Christmas Contest?" she blurted out.

"That's right," Mr. Henry said. "Are you Vanessa?"

Vanessa shrieked and began hopping around the living room.

Eight baffled pairs of eyes watched her, then turned back to Mr. Henry.

"What is this all about?" Mom asked.

"Didn't you see the commercial?" Vanessa cried. "You had to write a letter about the way your family was going to spend Christmas. And Mallory was saying how we had to have this old-style Christmas and all, so I entered us. I figured we'd be perfect."

"Your entry was sensational, Vanessa," Mr. Henry said. "I have to compliment you, Mrs. Pike. What a family. Eight children — and such a strong sense of closeness and traditional American values. Warmth, generosity, wholesomeness . . ."

As Mr. Henry searched for another word, Mom said, "What exactly does this contest entail? Do we have to buy anything?"

Mr. Henry chuckled and reached into his jacket pocket. "On the contrary, Mrs. Pike."

We all gathered around as Mr. Henry pulled out an envelope and removed a check from it.

I thought my jaw was going to hit the floor as I read it.

"Ten thousand dollars?" my mom said.

"*Yyyyyyyesss!*" Vanessa shouted.

"We're rich!" screamed Byron.

It was pandemonium in the monkey house. My siblings were bouncing off the walls.

I felt weak. I'd never seen a check that huge before. I wanted to hug Vanessa. I wanted to take back every mean thing I'd ever said to her.

I figured I'd wait until Mr. Henry left. Until we had the winning check in our house.

Mr. Henry unfolded some long, stapled-together papers, crowded with small type. "Of course, we'll need your authorization before we can start shooting," he said.

Claire gasped. "He *is* a policeman!"

"Not that kind of shooting," Vanessa said. "He means with TV cameras."

"In our house?" Byron asked.

"If your mom consents," Mr. Henry said. "You see, Mrs. Pike, I'm putting together a regular feature called 'Family First,' for our popular *Values AmericanStyle* show. By signing this contract, you become the focus of our gala winter special, to be broadcast a year from now. Over this holiday season, we will become part of your family, as it were. We'll videotape your old-fashioned Christmas preparations and let you share your joy with the entire Southern Connecticut community."

Mom looked at the contract. " 'Total access to the house'?" she read aloud.

"Only while you're here, of course," Mr. Henry said with a laugh. "We also may accompany you on Christmas-related outings. Of course, we'll keep equipment and personnel down to a minimum. We have no intention of diminishing your holiday enjoyment. After all, that would be counterproductive, wouldn't it?"

Adam nodded. "Yeah."

"What'd he say?" Nicky asked.

"I don't know," Adam murmured.

Mom sighed. "Let me hold on to this, Mr. Henry. We need to talk this out at a family meeting before we make any decisions."

"I respect that absolutely," Mr. Henry said. He folded up the check, put it back in his pocket, and took out a business card. "Call me at either my office or my home when you've made up your mind. I look forward to working with you. 'Bye, Vanessa! 'Bye, brothers and sisters! I hope to get to know you all personally."

" 'Bye," we replied.

Before Mr. Henry was even out of earshot, everyone spoke at once:

"We're stars!"

"Waaaaah-hoooo!"

"Where's the check?"

"Are we going to move to a palace?"

"Are we millionaires?"

"No, silly, thousandaires!"

"You're going to sign, right, Mom?"

"Mom?"

"Mom?"

My mother just shook her head and smiled patiently. "We'll discuss it after dinner."

For the next few hours, no one could talk about anything else. Adam and Byron argued about whether we should buy a Ferrari or a Porsche. Margo invented a butler named Grimsby, whom she and Claire began ordering around ("for practice," they said).

Vanessa had become an instant hero. Nicky gave her a stack of his comic books and magazines, opened to other contest offers. "Enter these, too," he demanded.

I wasn't sure how I felt about being on TV, but the money was definitely cool. I knew our family needed it. Awhile back my dad lost his job and was out of work for a few months.

We ended up spending all our savings before he found another job. Things are better now, but they've never been quite the same as before. Mom and Dad didn't make a big deal about it, but I knew how nervous they'd been about money.

As I helped Mom prepare dinner, I tried not to talk too much about the contest. Unfortunately, my siblings didn't feel the same way. Mom must have said "after dinner" about a million times.

Well, we didn't last. The moment Dad arrived home from work, he was mobbed by monkeys. In the interest of family peace, he and Mom decided to postpone the meal and call an early family meeting.

We gathered around the dining room table. Mom, Vanessa, and I described what had happened, and Dad looked carefully at the contract.

"Well, I see some red flags in terms of indemnity and privacy issues," said Dad. (Or something like that. He's a lawyer.)

"I don't see flags," Claire said, peering over his shoulder.

Nicky looked ready to cry. "Does that mean we can't do it?"

"I didn't say that," Dad replied. "But we have to be cautious. Think of all the people that'll be in our house."

"We always have a lot of people in the house," Adam insisted.

"Camera people all over the living room . . ." Mom said.

"*Yyyyyyes!*" Jordan exclaimed.

"Following us while we shop . . ." Dad conjectured.

"Everyone will want to know who we are," Vanessa said excitedly.

Byron was starry-eyed. "We'll give out autographs!"

Mom started laughing. Dad tried to keep a straight face, but that didn't last long.

"Well," Dad said with a sigh, "we certainly can use the money to put toward your educations."

"*Educations?*" Adam blurted out.

"What about a car?" Jordan said.

"Or a new house?" Margo asked.

Dad crossed his arms. "Look. If we do this, it is with the understanding that your mother and I have final fiduciary responsibility."

We stared at him blankly.

"In other words," Mom explained, "we'll give it a try, but leave the money matters to us."

Well, I don't need to tell you what the response to that was.

The joyful noise nearly shattered our windows.

CHAPTER 4

"You mean he showed you the check, then just took it away?" Kristy asked. "What a creep."

"He's going to give it back to them," Claudia said.

"If he hasn't left for Acapulco with it," Abby remarked.

Jessi giggled. "How could he?"

"Something like that happened in this book I read," Abby replied. "The bad guy killed the guy who had the check, and then disappeared to Mexico under an assumed name. But when the body floated up — "

"Abbyyyyy," I said warningly.

It was Wednesday afternoon. Everything with Channel 3 had been arranged the night before. My dad had called Mr. Henry immediately after the family meeting. By the end of the conversation, the contract was covered with crossouts, and stuff was scribbled in the

35

margins. But Dad and Mom signed it, and Dad said he'd mail it from his office.

"Will you still remember us when you're a big star, Mallory?" Stacey asked.

"Welllll . . ." I stuck my nose in the air. "*If* you contact me through my agent."

Kristy crumpled up an empty Fritos bag and threw it at me.

"Kidding!" I said.

"When are they going to start shooting?" Jessi asked.

"Saturday," I replied.

"Cool," Kristy said. "Can we watch?"

"I'm not sure," I said. "I mean, it's probably okay."

"The Pikes will have enough pressure without visitors, Kristy," Mary Anne remarked. (See how thoughtful she is?)

Kristy shrugged. "Okay. The next day, then."

"Is someone going to be, like, posted in your house twenty-four hours, to catch those special moments?" Claudia asked.

I laughed. "I don't think so."

"What happens if they show reruns?" Abby asked. "Do you get deciduals?"

Stacey howled. "*Deciduals?* Isn't that some kind of tree?"

"No, it's when you get paid for extra showings," Abby said.

"*Resid*uals," Claudia corrected her. "Rosie Wilder gets them for her commercials." (Rosie's one of our charges. She's only seven, but she acts professionally.)

"Yeah, those," Abby said. "Do you get them?"

"I don't know," I replied.

"Or maybe free products from the sponsor?" Stacey asked.

"For you and your friends!" Claudia exclaimed.

"Well, I — " I began.

"I know," Kristy cut in. "We could have our party at the Pikes'. Our first TV exposure."

Claudia rolled her eyes. "Uh, Kristy, I don't remember being invited."

"They want to capture Mallory's *family* life," Mary Anne said.

"Exactly." Kristy leaned forward. Her eyes were ablaze. "And friends are a big part of family life, right? It makes perfect sense for us to be in the film. The TV people will love it. And think of the fun we'll have. Think of the publicity."

"Aha!" Claudia cried. "I was waiting for that word."

"Look," Kristy barged on, "the show is called 'Family First.' Who will watch it? Families. What is the BSC client base? Huh?"

"Families," said Claudia, Stacey, and Abby in a monotone.

Kristy looked at me triumphantly. "Well? How about asking your mom and dad?"

"Okay," I said. "But it's not only them. The production company made my parents sign this big contract with all kinds of rules. I don't know what's allowed and what's not. I'll ask, though."

"All riiiiight!" Kristy replied.

The jangling of the phone cut off our conversation. Just in time, too. A few minutes more and Kristy would have been planning a weekly primetime show and a feature film.

Claudia snatched up the receiver. "Baby-sitters Club, Home of the Stars!" she said. "No, just joking, Mrs. Braddock. Tuesday afternoon? I'll see who's available and call you right back. 'Bye."

" 'Home of the Stars'?" Kristy said, scowling.

"Should I have said 'Future Stars'?" Claudia asked.

Mary Anne was scanning the record book. "Tuesday's pretty crowded. I've got the Arnold twins; Mal's home with Claire, Margo, and Vanessa; Jessi's got ballet class — "

"Nope, canceled," Jessi piped up. "Madame Noelle has zee flu. I'll do the job."

"Okay," Mary Anne said, filling in Jessi's name.

As Claudia called Mrs. Braddock back, Stacey reached into her bag and pulled out a copy of the *Stoneybrook News*. "Look what was in the paper yesterday."

She held up a folded-out page for us to read:

YOUR PLACE FOR ONE-STOP HOLIDAY SHOPPING.
STONEYBROOK MANOR
PRESENTS ITS FIRST ANNUAL
CHRISTMAS BOUTIQUE
CLOTHING * TOYS * BOOKS * BAKERY GOODS
AND MUCH, MUCH MORE!
ALL PROCEEDS TO BENEFIT THE MANOR
DECEMBER 15–19, 5:00–9:00 P.M.

* * *

Volunteers needed
Donations gratefully accepted
Mrs. Kronauer
JL5-6100

"Let's call them," Jessi said. "We said we wanted to donate stuff."

"All in favor say 'Aye,' " Kristy called out.

"Kristyyyy, we know we're all in favor," Claudia said.

"I know, but it should be official," Kristy replied.

"Aye!" I said.

"Nose!" Abby piped up.

"Ear!" Mary Anne added.

Kristy shook her head. "No respect."

Jessi picked up the receiver and tapped out the number.

"Ask them what they need most," Stacey suggested.

"Hello, may I speak to Mrs. Kronauer? . . . Oh, hi! Uh-huh, my name's Jessi Ramsey. I belong to this group, the Baby-sitters Club, and we'd like to find out what we can donate to the Christmas Boutique. . . . Oh? . . . Sure we do. . . . Uh-huh. . . . No problem. I'll ask and call you back. . . . 'Bye."

"What was that all about?" Kristy asked as Claud hung up.

"For their gala opening," Jessi replied, "they want to offer free child care for shoppers. Mrs. Kronauer was going to ask volunteers at the Manor, but she needs as many people as possible for sales. So she asked if we would do the sitting."

"That would be fun," Mary Anne said.

"And great publicity," Kristy added.

"Krist*yyyyyy*," Claudia and Stacey said together.

"She also needs baked goods, because they'll go fast," Jessi continued. "And any unusual crafts — things that people might not find in stores."

"I found these great doll patterns in a magazine," Mary Anne said.

"My sister and I can make the most amazing candy-bar cake," Abby volunteered.

"I'll help!" Claudia said quickly.

"I said 'Make it.' " Abby grinned slyly. "Not 'Eat it.' "

"Right." Claudia nodded. "Maybe I'll stick to my art project."

"I can unload some of my brothers' and sisters' decorations," I said. "At the rate they're going, we'll have enough for a warehouse."

"I'll ask my mom if her publishing company can donate books," Abby suggested.

"What about Anna?" Kristy asked. "Would she volunteer to play a violin piece on opening day? You know, for background music?"

"Whoa, hold on," Jessi said. "First things first. Should I tell Mrs. Kronauer we'll babysit on the fifteenth?"

Mary Anne looked at the calendar. "At this point, we're all open."

"Let's do it," Kristy said.

"Yeeeeaaa!" Claudia, Jessi, and I blurted out.

"All in flavor?" said Abby.

Dumb joke, but we broke up laughing.

Stoneybrook Manor wasn't going to know what hit it.

CHAPTER 5

Thursday

I really meant well. I thought I had a fantastic idea for the boutique. I figured Haley and Matt would be just as excited as I was.

Honestly, if Mallory hadn't bailed me out, today would have been a disaster. I feel much better now. I did learn a valuable lesson. I now that I will never again go shopping with my aunt Cecelia....

"Make up your mind, dear," Jessi's aunt Cecelia said. "My feet are killing me."

Crouched over a bin at the Stoneybrook Thrift Shop, Jessi picked a dusty wooden frame. "This is perfect."

"Jessica Ramsey, do you think your father and mother are made out of money?" Aunt Cecelia scolded.

"Look at the price," Jessi said.

Aunt Cecelia slid her glasses down her nose. The sales clerk wandered over, smiling blandly. "Most of the frames are under a dollar," he said. "They're a little damaged."

"Mm-hm, well, then, all right," Aunt Cecelia grumbled.

Aunt Cecelia is Mr. Ramsey's sister. She lives with Jessi's family. In case you haven't noticed, she can be a little, well, difficult.

"Do you have any small, colorful toy things that I could glue around the frames?" Jessi asked the salesman. "You know, to decorate them?"

"Hmmm, small toy things," the man repeated.

"Honestly, Jessica." Aunt Cecelia harrumphed.

"Let me take you to our tchotchke collection," the man said.

"Your *what*?" Jessi said.

"Tchotchkes. Little decorative items. Stuff you never know what to do with."

The man led Jessi and Aunt Cecelia to a corner of the store. A bookshelf there was crammed with tiny figurines made of ceramic and plastic and wood.

On the floor below it was a box marked JUNQUE. "Like the fancy spelling?" the man said with a chortle.

Corny, huh? But the box was perfect. It was chock-full of fun miniatures — people, horses, dogs, sleds, golf clubs, soda bottles, baby blocks, you name it. "These are so cute!" Jessi exclaimed.

The man smiled. "I'll let you have the box for three dollars."

"Three dollars?" Aunt Cecelia asked.

"Okay, two-fifty," the man replied. Out of the side of his mouth, he said to Jessi, "Your sister drives a hard bargain."

Now Aunt Cecelia chortled. And she stayed in a good mood during the rest of the trip.

Boy, was Jessi psyched when she arrived at Haley's and Matt's. She took some last-minute baby-sitting instructions from Mr. and Mrs. Braddock. Then, as they rushed out to a meeting, she announced, "I have a surprise project."

She carefully signed the words to Matt. He is profoundly deaf, which means he cannot hear even the slightest sound. By now, most of us BSC members know some American Sign Language, but Jessi's the best at it.

"Today," Jessi continued, "we are going to make designer frames."

Matt stared at her quizzically.

Haley looked as if Jessi had just suggested laying bathroom tile. "Boring. I wanted to play Mille Bornes."

Pffffffft. (That was the air leaking out of Jessi's balloon.)

What did she do? Cry her eyes out? Beg Haley and Matt to change their minds? Call Aunt Cecelia and tell her she was right about the money?

None of the above. I, Mallory Pike, came to the rescue. I had just called Kristy to tell her that my parents had agreed to host the BSC party (yea!). Only my sisters were with me (everyone else had run off to shop and play), and they really wanted company. So I invited Mary Anne and the Arnold twins to come over. And then I called Jessi.

Rrrrrring!

"Braddock residence," Jessi said glumly.

"Jessi? Are you okay?" I asked.

"They hate my idea. I spent an hour listening to Aunt Cecelia tell me how much money I was wasting, and it turned out she was right."

"Bring the stuff over here," I suggested. "We're doing art projects for the boutique. Mary Anne just called. She's coming over with Marilyn and Carolyn."

When Jessi mentioned the idea to Haley and Matt, I could hear their squeals of excitement.

We said good-bye. Haley and Matt bundled up. Jessi put on her down coat, clutched her unopened thrift-shop bag, and led the kids to our house.

When they arrived at our door, my sisters and I were huddled over the kitchen table, hard at work.

"Hi!" Jessi called out, stepping into the vestibule. "What are you doing?"

"Envelopes," Claire replied without looking up.

"Collages," Margo chimed in.

"Ooh, I *love* collages," Haley said.

She and Matt dropped their coats on the floor and rushed in.

Claire was gluing sequins and beads and colorful strips of paper onto sheets of colored construction paper, then folding and taping the paper into pockets. Vanessa and Margo were cutting out pictures from a stack of magazines and carefully placing them in piles.

"Take some scissors," Vanessa urged Haley. "This pile is Christmas pictures, this one is animals, and this one is baby stuff."

Matt signed something to Haley. "Can Matt cut out sports pictures?" Haley asked.

Margo made a face. "You're supposed to hang these in a *baby's* room."

"Can't babies like sports?" I asked.

Muttering, Margo pushed some magazines and scissors toward Matt. Jessi pulled over a chair for him, and he gleefully went to work.

The kitchen echoed with snips, snaps, and rips.

A few minutes later, the bell rang. (Mary Anne's the only person polite enough to ring instead of barge inside.)

"We brought origami!" Marilyn Arnold called out as I opened the door. (Or maybe it was Carolyn. It's hard to tell.)

"Ooh, can I help?" Whoosh. Away flew Margo, the collages quickly forgotten.

Jessi and I helped clear some space for the three origami makers. (One nice thing about a large family is that you have big tables.)

Jessi, Mary Anne, and I chatted for a while. Then we put together a snack plate of fruit, cheese, and crackers and set it on the table.

Big mistake.

"Margo!" Claire yelled. She was staring in

disgust at one of her envelopes, where an orange lump sat in the middle of a drying glop of Elmer's glue. "She dropped cheese on my envelope to Santa!"

Haley cracked up. "So? He can feed it to Rudolph."

"Rudolph the red-nosed reindeer," Vanessa sang. "Liked to eat some rotten cheese . . ."

Haley signed something to Matt, and he laughed so hard he sent a spray of cracker crumbs across the table.

"Eeeeeww!" Carolyn cried.

"Say it, don't spray it!" Marilyn said.

"And if you ever pet him, you will surely catch his fleas," Vanessa continued.

"Here," Claire said, squeezing an orange slice over Matt's pile of pictures.

Matt roared with anger.

"Guys! *Guys!*" Jessi yelled. She inserted her fingers in her mouth and let out a whistle.

It wasn't as loud as Kristy's monster whistles, but it did the trick. The table fell silent, more or less.

I whisked away the snack plate.

"Hey!" Haley protested.

"Later," I said. "When you're ready for a break."

The kids quietly returned to work.

Jessi, Mary Anne, and I gabbed some more.

We had fun watching origami stars, chairs, boxes, and animals take shape. Carolyn made the coolest triceratops.

After a while Mary Anne noticed the thrift-shop bag. "What's that?" she asked.

"Nothing," Jessi said. "Just a rejected project. Frame-making."

"Can I see?"

Jessi brought the bag into the dining room. She dumped the frames and figurines onto the table.

"Wow," Mary Anne said.

"What I wanted to do," Jessi said, picking up the roll of Christmas paper, "was glue strips of this on the frames, and then glue these tchotchkes onto the paper."

"Glue these *what?*" Mary Anne said.

"Things," Jessi explained. "You know, for a baby's frame, you line it with blocks and milk bottles and rattles." She picked up a tiny plastic baseball bat and miniature ballet slippers. "For older kids, a sports theme or a dance theme."

"Jessi, that's one of your best ideas!" I exclaimed.

"What is?" Marilyn asked from the kitchen. She wandered into the dining room, followed by Margo.

Jessi began covering one of the frames with

shiny silver paper. Carefully she glued it in place. Then she glued on teeny toy trains and trucks.

"Cooool!" Now Haley was in the room watching.

In a moment, the kitchen was empty. Matt insisted on putting together a sports frame. Vanessa wanted to handle the dance theme.

One by one, the kids sat at the dining room table. Jessi, Mary Anne, and I circulated, helping them pick things from the tchotchke collection.

You should have seen Jessi's face. She was glowing.

"What would Aunt Cecelia say now?" I asked.

Jessi looked at me very seriously. "What she always says when she's wrong."

"What's that?" Mary Anne asked.

" 'My feet are killing me,' " Jessi replied.

CHAPTER 6

"Is that them?"

Claire's voice startled me awake. I looked at my dresser clock.

Ten minutes to seven.

I rubbed my eyes and sat up. The room was dark. Outside, the street was dark. The world was fast asleep.

Inside the Pike house, however, it might as well have been midafternoon. I could hear the triplets downstairs, fighting with each other and Nicky. Vanessa was thumping down the stairs, singing to the tune of "Twinkle Twinkle Little Star": "I am going to be a star, and I'll buy a brand-new car."

"Mom! Dad! I think they're here!" That was Claire. She whizzed past my bedroom, on her way to my parents'. "I heard a noise outside!"

I looked outside again. Across the street, a neighbor's car was pulling away from the curb.

I stood up and stumbled groggily to my

door. As I opened it onto the second-floor hallway, I heard my dad's voice rumbling, "Sweetheart, they're not scheduled to come until ten o'clock."

"They" were the Channel 3 TV crew.

Yes, it was Saturday. My family and I were about to enter television history.

Did I feel up to the challenge?

You bet!

My heart was beating so hard I thought my ribs would crack. I gripped the banister tightly as I started to descend. My dreams were still floating around in my head. In them, we Pikes had become worldwide celebrities. People were watching us in New York City apartments and California beach houses. Our faces peered out identically from hundreds of screens in TV/video stores. Shoppers chased us for autographs in the mall. Cars and mini-vans and RVs with South Dakota license plates clogged Slate Street, rolling slooowly by our house with their windows down, so the passengers could gawk. Dad and Mom came home daily with stacks of movie offers.

Claire's voice had awakened me just as we'd been about to accept starring roles in a hilarious new comedy in which our parents leave all of us home alone by mistake.

Do you think I was taking this too seriously?

Nahhhh.

I shuffled downstairs and into the kitchen. Mom, Dad, and Claire were right behind me.

The table was crowded with open cereal boxes and half-finished bowls of soggy cereal. The triplets and Nicky were gathered by the front window, fully dressed, jabbering excitedly.

"Guys," Dad called out, "we have a few hours, so let's calm down and eat breakfast."

I tried. I poured myself a bowl of cereal, but I could barely eat. Boy, was I nervous.

As I gazed listlessly into my Raisin Bran, a lock of hair fell across my eyes.

Yikes! I hadn't thought about my hair at all. It was a mop. A thick, red, bushy mop. I hate the way I look in photos when my hair is too long.

Why hadn't I gotten a haircut?

"Mom," I said. "I have a major emergency."

Good old Mom. She understood. After breakfast she took me downtown, where I had a quick haircut that didn't look too horrible.

We were finished at twenty minutes to ten. On our way home, my heart raced. I knew just what to expect. Once, when I was visiting New York City, I spotted a TV shoot on one of the streets. The curbside had been roped off to parked cars, and three enormous vans sat there, all hooked to an electric generator. Their windows were curtained and wooden steps led from the door to the sidewalk. Wires snaked all around, taped down to the pavement. Dozens of workers hauled equipment from a truck. Just beyond them was a huge table that overflowed with food. It's one of my strongest NYC memories.

When we arrived home, a Channel 3 minivan was parked in front of our house.

Yes, *a*.

Yes, *minivan*.

No trucks. No bustle. No banquet.

Thunk, went my heart as it sank.

But I could deal with it. I mean, *duh*, this wasn't network TV, or a feature film.

Maybe next year.

Mom parked. I adjusted my hair. I took a deep breath. Mom gave me an encouraging smile, and we walked inside.

"And for Christmas I want a TV set for my own room and a computer that does games and this new doll that you can burp because she's so cute and do you have a daughter?"

Claire was talking a mile a minute into a video camera. The man who was holding the camera looked about ready to crack up. "Uh, no, I don't," he said. "But go ahead. Tell me what else you want for Christmas."

Neither of them noticed us come in. We walked into the dining room. Coats were draped over the chairs and empty paper coffee cups lined the windowsills. Several black leather bags lay open on the floor, and a tripod stood alone by the table like an abandoned statue.

A tingle shot through me. This was it. Showtime!

The rest of my family, Mr. Henry, and a camerawoman were in the kitchen. The triplets, Vanessa, Margo, and Nicky were busily setting out baking stuff. Pow was hanging out, looking befuddled, wagging his tail ferociously.

Dad was standing by the kitchen window when Mom and I entered. "Hi, sweetie!" he said. "You look beautiful."

"Thanks." I walked over to him. Lowering my voice to a whisper, I asked, "Did we get the check?" (Hey, important questions first.)

"Yes," Dad whispered back.

We gave each other thumbs-ups.

"Mallory, Pallory!" Margo yelled as she dumped flour into a bowl. "We are having so much fun!"

A cloud of smoke poofed up. Margo shrieked. Pow barked noisily. Dad jumped to the rescue.

"Get the smoke, Jeannie," Mr. Henry mumbled to the camerawoman. "That's it."

"Milk in the batter! Milk in the batter!" Vanessa sang, holding out a milk carton to the camera.

Splat!

"Eeeeeeew!" Jordan screamed. "Nicky dropped eggshells in the bowl!"

"That's great, that's great, can we get a shot of the shells? Maybe get the dog over here, to sniff them?" Mr. Henry said to the cameraman. "Excuse me, uh, Adam."

"I'm Byron," said Byron.

He moved aside, letting the camerawoman zoom in on the shell floating around in the egg goo.

"Mm, crrrunchy!" Margo said.

"Take it out, Nicky," Jordan commanded.

Nicky looked at the bowl in horror. "I'm not putting my fingers in that!"

Saved by Dad again. I have hardly ever seen him laughing so hard.

"Back up, Jeannie," Mr. Henry murmured. "Get the whole family."

RAWF!

Jeannie had backed up right into Pow's front paw.

"Oooh, I'm sorry," Jeannie said.

"Cut!" Mr. Henry said.

"Hey! Can I help?" Claire squealed, running into the kitchen. As she passed me, she grinned from ear to ear. "I'm going to be the star," she said confidentially. "Todd said so."

"Todd who?" I asked.

"Him." She pointed to the cameraman, who had followed behind her. "He's the director."

Mr. Henry's eyebrows went way up. "Oh?"

"I said, *assistant*." The cameraman laughed nervously. "What are you guys making?"

"Gingerbread men," Nicky said. "I mean, people."

"And sugar cookies," Vanessa added.

"Decorated with faces and buttons," Margo explained.

"And chocolate chip cookies," Adam said.

"With our super secret recipe!" Jordan exclaimed.

Nicky nodded. "Yeah. Twice as much brown sugar as white, so they're chewier."

"Nick*yyyyy*, now it's not a secret!" Adam scolded.

"Let's roll it," Mr. Henry said.

"Is all this stuff for you?" Todd asked, hoisting the camera to his shoulders.

"Uh-uh," Vanessa said. Smiling woodenly into the camera, she continued in a singsong voice, "These will be gifts for all our kind friends and neighbors, to spread good cheer and the spirit of a warm, old-fashioned Christmas."

"Make me barf," Adam muttered.

"Adaaaaam!" Vanessa snapped. She looked

pleadingly at Mr. Henry. "Can we redo that?"

"Cut!" Mr. Henry said. "No problem. We'll stay as long as this takes."

"How many cookies are you planning to bake?" Jeannie asked.

"Thirty dozen," Mom answered.

"That's three hundred and sixty," Vanessa volunteered.

Todd almost dropped his camera.

But he and Jeannie and Mr. Henry stayed in there the whole time, through oven openings and closings, through burnt batches and cookie swipings, and even a food fight or two.

It was so much fun.

That's show biz.

CHAPTER 7

After school on Tuesday, Jessi, Kristy, Mary Anne, and I went to Stoneybrook Manor for our appointment with Mrs. Kronauer. Jessi had set it up at Monday's BSC meeting.

I was back on Earth, more or less. The shoot had gone pretty well, with just a few goof-ups. Margo had flung some cookie dough onto Jeannie's camera lens. Todd had spilled some coffee on the dining room carpet. Pow had managed to eat a big hunk of raw dough and became sick. But all in all, we'd had a great time. Believe it or not, we'd made thirty dozen cookies. (Dad and I ended up making the last few batches, when everyone else lost interest.)

The crew was going to return on Wednesday. At school, everyone wanted to know how the shoot had gone — friends, teachers, even kids I'd never met. I had to answer the same questions over and over. But you know what? I didn't mind at all.

Fame was okay.

I was in a pretty terrific mood as I walked to the Manor with my friends. The day was warm for December, sunny and clear. A few of the elderly tenants were taking walks in front of the building with their nurses. They stopped and waved to us as we approached.

Stoneybrook Manor is a long, modern, one-story building with lots of windows. As we stepped through the revolving door, we entered a small, crowded lobby. Diagonally from the door to the main hallway, a threadbare streak had been worn into the floor by shoes and canes and wheelchairs. Visiting hours were ending, and as families filed out, nurses bustled around them.

I realized how rundown and small the place was. No wonder they needed to raise some money.

A trim, white-haired woman with sharp blue eyes was standing in the open door of a large room off the hallway. When she spotted us, she smiled brightly. She was dressed in a tartan flannel skirt and simple white blouse. Her shoulders were slightly stooped, but she walked toward us with a lively bounce. "Pardon me, is one of you Jessica Ramsey?"

"That's me," Jessi said, offering her hand. "And you're Mrs. Kronauer?"

"That's me!" Mrs. Kronauer replied. "Delighted to meet you, and thanks so much for agreeing to help."

Jessi introduced us all around.

"Are you Joseph Pike's granddaughter?" Mrs. Kronauer asked when she heard my name.

"Grand-niece," I said.

"Well, I'm sure he'd love to see you after we're finished."

"Really? But visiting hours — "

"Not to worry. We're a group home, not an army base."

Behind Mrs. Kronauer, a group of residents was helping two custodians carry folding tables into the large room. "By the way, we're going to have the boutique over there in our rec room," she continued. "In the back of the room is an alcove, where we plan to set up our special section for children's items. Now, let me show you the room I have in mind for your baby-sitting."

She led us down the hallway to a smaller, carpeted room. It was cozy, like a living room, with two sofas and a TV. A couple of residents were chatting away on the sofas, and they smiled as we walked in.

"This is one of our lounges," Mrs. Kronauer said. "I can arrange for it to be free on the fifteenth."

"Looks great," I said.

"Comfortable," Mary Anne remarked.

"No sharp objects," Jessi said.

Kristy gazed around the room. "I'll bring along some plastic plugs for the electrical outlets."

Mrs. Kronauer grinned. "You are top-notch baby-sitters, I can tell. I'll be happy to supply some toys, books, and games. We have them on hand for visiting grandchildren . . . and great-grandchildren!"

"And if you could spare them, maybe a table and chairs," Mary Anne said. "For art projects."

"I'll ask the custodian," Mrs. Kronauer replied. "Now, we'll need you for four hours, from five o'clock to nine. Of course, we'll have food for you and the children . . ."

As we talked more about details, Mrs. Kronauer walked us back to the lobby.

Smmmack!

The sound from the rec room startled us. We looked inside and saw that a folding table had collapsed onto the floor. An elderly man was bending over it.

Mrs. Kronauer rushed toward him. "Are you all right, Mr. Mead?"

Mr. Mead was fine. Kristy ran to him and helped him lift the table up. Jessi, Mary Anne, and I helped adjust the legs.

Then Kristy darted off and helped set up another table.

"Dear, you don't need to do that," Mrs. Kronauer said.

"I don't mind," Kristy called over her shoulder.

Mary Anne and Jessi were now wandering over to a table by the corner, where several residents were preparing decorations and a big banner.

One of the women in the group pulled up two chairs. As she gestured for my friends to sit, Mary Anne turned to Mrs. Kronauer. "Do you mind if we help?"

"Mind?" Mrs. Kronauer smiled. "Goodness, you girls are already part of the family."

"Speaking of family," I said, "is it okay if I see my uncle Joe now?"

"Of course. I'll take you to his room."

I told Kristy, Mary Anne, and Jessi where I'd be. Then I followed Mrs. Kronauer to Room 14.

"THAT'S RIGHT! NINE OUT OF TEN DOCTORS SURVEYED RECOMMEND SKIN-SILK CLEANSING CREAM FOR EFFECTIVE ACNE REMOVAL! JUST CALL ONE-EIGHT

HUNDRED-ZIT-GONE FOR YOUR FREE SAMPLE!"

I could hear Uncle Joe's TV blaring halfway down the hall. When I looked inside the room, Uncle Joe was sitting in bed, smiling and looking out the window, while the pimple commercial gave way to a heavy metal video.

Somehow I kept a straight face. That was not what I expected him to be watching.

"Mr. Pike?" Mrs. Kronauer said, almost yelling. *"It's your grand-niece."*

"Hmmm?" Uncle Joe said, turning toward us.

"It's Mallory," Mrs. Kronauer repeated.

Uncle Joe looked at me. For a moment, my stomach knotted. Did he recognize me? I couldn't tell. Alzheimer's can rob a person's memory so fast.

He didn't say anything to me, but he glared at Mrs. Kronauer. "What?" he yelled back.

A guitar solo seemed to ricochet around the room.

"This is your grand-niece, Mallory!" Mrs. Kronauer tried again.

"Well, of course it is!" Uncle Joe snapped. "I'm not blind!"

Mrs. Kronauer's smile tightened. "Um," she said, "I'll leave you two to chat."

As soon as she left, Uncle Joe gave me a

wink. A smile crept across his face.

I cracked up.

"Turn the TV down, will you, Laurie?"

At least that was what I thought he said. But it was hard to tell with the noise. I turned the volume almost to Off. "I didn't know you liked music videos," I said.

"I don't pay attention to it," Uncle Joe said, waving dismissively at the TV. "It drives Connor out of the room, though, so it can't be all bad."

Mr. Connor is the name of Uncle Joe's roommate. (Why does the word *long-suffering* pop into my brain when I think of him?)

"What brings you to this place?" Uncle Joe continued. "Little old me?"

"Well, um, my friends and I are going to help out with the Christmas Boutique." Boy, did I feel guilty saying that. I mean, it was the truth, but it made it sound as if I hadn't wanted to see him.

Uncle Joe nodded. "Connor's working on that." He looked as if he wanted to say more, but his eyes wandered over to the TV.

"Are you?" I asked. "I mean, working on it?"

"No, no," he said softly. "Could you please get me my drink, Laurie?"

That time the mistake was clear. I was too

embarrassed to say anything. I reached for a half-finished cup of juice on his dresser and gave it to him.

Uncle Joe's hands shook as he took it from me. As he sipped, a thin trail of juice dribbled down his cheek. I grabbed a tissue and gently wiped it off.

Uncle Joe was such a confusing guy. On the one hand, he could be so gruff and cranky. But on the other hand, he seemed so frail and alone.

We didn't talk much longer. But when we said good-bye, he called me Mallory, not Laurie. And he did remember about our Christmas invitation. That made me feel a little better.

I met Jessi and Mary Anne in the rec room. Things were going smoothly in there. One of the residents, a man named Mr. Rubin, was playing an old upright piano in a corner.

We said good-bye to Mrs. Kronauer and walked home together.

Of the three of our houses, mine is the farthest from the Manor. So I was pretty tired as I turned up Slate Street. And I did not expect to see the Channel 3 van parked in front of my house.

What was it doing there? I ran the rest of the way home.

I pushed open the front door, but Mr. Henry

blocked my entrance. "Cut!" he called into the room. Then, to me, he said, "Come in a moment, Valerie."

"Mallory," I corrected him. (Was my name so difficult? Or was he in the first stages of Alzheimer's, too?)

"Sorry," Mr. Henry said. "Just stand with your parents."

Mom and Dad were near the fireplace. "Why are they here?" I asked them.

"They wanted to redo a few things that didn't come out well," Mom replied. "Plus add some standard generic stuff they can splice in later."

"Like this," Dad added, gesturing toward the staircase.

Jeannie was standing near the base of the stairs, looking up toward the second floor. "Action!" Mr. Henry yelled.

Suddenly Pow shot downstairs. The triplets followed, running a little stiffly, as if they were being tested for coordination. Nicky was next, then Margo.

Before Vanessa and Claire could descend, Mr. Henry yelled, "Cut! Very nice, kids. But could you do it again, only yuk it up a bit? You know, whoopee! Christmas is just around the corner!" He started dancing around foolishly.

"Like that?" Nicky said, looking horrified.

"Come on, birdbrain," Adam said, pushing Nicky upstairs.

"Can I slide down?" Margo asked.

"You've never done it!" Byron said.

"I can!" Margo insisted.

They all scrambled upstairs, Margo holding Pow. Jordan then solemnly announced, "Actors and dog ready on the set."

"Okay . . . action!" Mr. Henry shouted.

"Whoooooo!" the triplets hollered, barreling downstairs. They sounded more warlike than happy.

Margo slid down the bannister but became scared. She stopped in the middle, fell off, and started crying.

"Cut!" Mr. Henry called.

Mom and Dad ran to help Margo. I could see we were in for a long evening.

CHAPTER 8

Nestor joined us the next night.

Nestor was another cameraman. The Channel 3 crew was going with us to Washington Mall. For a job like this, they needed an expanded staff.

Why were we, the all-natural, old-fashioned, make-your-own-holiday Pikes going to a mall? Supplies, for one thing. We had run out of tape, staples, and glue. We had to buy gifts, too. Let's face it, some of them we just could not make, such as books and socks and underwear.

But the main reason we were going was because of North Pole Village. That's where Santa greets local kids every year.

Who still believes in Santa Claus? Well, just Claire, and even she's suspicious. But you don't have to believe in Santa to love North Pole Village.

Every year after Thanksgiving, it appears

inside Lear's department store overnight, like magic. Actually, it's set up by workers behind a high, makeshift wall, decorated to look like a humongous Christmas present. When you step past Wonderland Gate, you follow a winding pathway through a snowy fantasyland. Christmas carols play over the speakers as you walk past hard-working puppet elves, clanking machinery, gingerbread houses, a reindeer stable, a post office stuffed with mail, and tinkling bells. Over it all is a blue-black rooftop with glittering stars.

Just thinking about it, I have goosebumps.

As usual, we drove to the mall in both station wagons. I was in Dad's car with Vanessa, Margo, and Claire. My brothers were in Mom's car. Mr. Henry, Jeannie, Todd, and Nestor followed in the Channel 3 van.

"I hope I do not cause a spillage," Vanessa recited, "when we have ice cream sodas after North Pole Village."

"We're having ice cream sodas?" Claire exclaimed.

Dad shot Vanessa a Look.

"I meant to say *if*," Vanessa quickly added.

As soon as Dad parked in the Washington Mall lot, we practically leaped out of the car.

"I call I'm first to see Santa!" Claire yelled.

"Clai-*aire*." Margo giggled. "He's not . . . you know."

"So?" Claire replied. "He's still a celebrity!"

"Wonderful!" Mr. Henry's voice made us all turn. He was trotting toward us, with Nestor close behind. "I loved that. Could you do it again for the camera?"

Claire looked at Margo. "Do what?" Margo asked.

"The part about Santa being a celebrity," Mr. Henry said. "Do you remember the words?"

Nestor raised the camera and pointed it at Claire. "Go ahead, say, 'I call first dibs on Santa!' " he said.

"What's a dib?" Claire asked.

Mom's car had just parked, and the boys were scrambling out. "First come, first served!" Adam shouted, darting for the entrance.

"Heeeyy!" Claire shrieked. "No fair!"

She ran after Adam. Dad ran after her. Margo, Vanessa, and I ran after Dad. Nestor, Mr. Henry, Jeannie, and Todd ran after them.

You can imagine what we looked like as we entered the mall. A thundering herd. Stores emptied. Cameras flashed. Diners in the food court dropped their sandwiches and came running to see us.

Okay, I'm exaggerating. But not by much.

People were staring. I could see little kids tugging at their parents, whispering questions. Nestor and Jeannie were following our every move with their cameras.

I felt so self-conscious. Even with my new haircut.

"Where to, guys?" Mr. Henry asked my mom and dad.

Dad looked a little bewildered. "Well, I wanted to stop in BookCenter for a minute, and then I suppose we'll to go North Pole Village — "

"YEEEEEEEEAAAAA!" screamed my brothers and sisters.

Their voices echoed. I was so embarrassed.

The cameras followed us into BookCenter. In the kids' section, I found the coolest book. It was called *Christmas Tree Farm*, by Sandra Jordan, about a real-life family who goes to a Christmas tree farm and chops its own tree to bring home.

This, of course, gave me another perfect idea for the Pike family old-fashioned Christmas. I begged Mom and Dad to let me buy the book. (They did. I guess with the cameras on them, they couldn't disagree.)

You should have seen my siblings as we walked toward Lear's. Claire and Margo kept turning and grinning at the cameras. Adam and Byron were practicing Ninja moves, shouting "Hyahh!" at the top of their lungs. Jordan was walking in front of us all, his chest puffed out and his fists clenched, as if he were our great warrior leader.

Mr. Henry walked to the side of us, out of camera range. He was eyeing the crowd sternly. Like those Secret Service agents who walk everywhere with the First Family.

We filed into Lear's. Over the doors was a huge sign that said WELCOME TO LEAR'S, HOME OF NORTH POLE VILLAGE.

I began to feel excited. Inside the store, bells jingled and carols played. Thick green and red carpets crisscrossed the floors. Long pine garlands, intertwined with lights, hung from the ceiling.

Another sign for North Pole Village pointed us to the up escalator. The triplets started racing.

"What floor is Santa on?" Mr. Henry asked.

"The second," I replied.

"Kids!" Mr. Henry shouted after the triplets. "Can we do this together?"

Too late. They were halfway up. "I'll get them," Mom said. "The rest of you stay here."

Mr. Henry mumbled something to the camera people. Jeannie and Todd headed for the escalators themselves.

"We'll do an establishing shot on the escalator," Mr. Henry explained to Dad. "I'll need all of you, crowded but enjoying yourselves. We'll cover it from three perspectives. Nestor will shoot you from this floor. Todd will catch you at the top. Jeannie will ride the down escalator and tape you in motion."

"Right," Dad said solemnly. "Did you hear that, everybody?"

Five blank faces.

"Follow me," Mr. Henry ordered.

The first time we went up, Margo and Adam were arguing. Mr. Henry called "Cut!" and made us go back and do it again.

The second time, a family of four squeezed onto the escalator in the midst of us.

On take three, Nestor wasn't ready.

On take four, we looked as if we were at a funeral.

Between our fifth and sixth times, I think, a little boy approached us with an autograph book and pen. "Who are you?" he asked.

"Jordan Pike and his family," Jordan announced proudly, reaching for the pen.

The boy's face fell. "Never heard of you," he said, snapping his book shut and walking back to his mother.

We taped the escalator bit seven times.

Yes, seven. How frustrated were we by then? Totally. Claire was almost in tears.

More shoppers were watching now. I couldn't help thinking about my dream. About the crowds, the fame, the autograph seekers.

The dream had felt fantastic. Just then,

though, I felt like an amoeba under a microscope.

As we walked toward North Pole Village, a group of helpers in elf uniforms were singing "It Came Upon a Midnight Clear." They sounded fantastic. I started to feel cheery again.

The line snaked all the way out the entrance and down the hall, but that was okay. It would be worth the wait.

Todd chuckled. "Uh-oh. Looks like we're going overtime."

But Mr. Henry led us right to the entrance. There, a friendly-looking elf helper was greeting visitors and giving out North Pole Village souvenir pins.

"Pardon me," Mr. Henry said to her. "I'd like to bring these people to Santa briefly — "

A woman at the head of the line spoke up loudly. "I'm sorry, sir, but we've all been waiting a long time."

Mr. Henry smiled stiffly. "I'm sure you have." He turned back to the helper, who looked, well, help*less*. "We'll only be a minute. I'm with Channel Three and — "

"I don't care who you're with, pal," boomed a man waiting in line with his family. "Fair is fair."

"The end of the line is back here!" someone called from down the hallway.

A tall man in a dark blue suit jogged to Mr. Henry and said, "Sir, I'm going to have to ask you to leave — "

Mr. Henry glared at him. "Who are you?"

"I'm the assistant manager," the man answered.

"Well, you talk to Mr. Bouchard, your boss," Mr. Henry insisted. "He issued me a permit, and he told me we had unlimited access."

"I understand, but access does not mean — "

Dad cut in. "It's all right, Mr. Henry, we're happy to wait our turn."

"No, we're not!" Claire declared, stamping her feet. "That line is too long!"

What a time for a tantrum.

Claire was screaming. Mr. Henry was arguing with the assistant manager. The assistant manager pulled out a cellular phone and called someone. The triplets started bothering Dad. The people in line looked furious.

By the time the manager, Mr. Bouchard, ran to us, it seemed as if the whole store were watching us.

While Mr. Henry and Mr. Bouchard talked, Dad and Mom snuck all of us back to the end of the line.

Before long, Mr. Henry joined us. "Sorry, folks," he said. "They're making it a little hard. We will have to wait in line. And because of the length, we won't be allowed to do any retakes. If you'd rather, we could shoot you all shopping first, then come back to North Pole Village later on."

"I want to stay," Nicky said.

"Let's go to the video store," Adam insisted.

"Yeah," Vanessa said. "We need a VCR."

"We have one," Mom retorted.

"But we can't tape off a tape," Vanessa explained. "And now we have ten thousand dollars — "

"I want a computer!" Byron said.

"A dirt bike!" Jordan called out.

"A CD player!" Margo shouted.

"North Pole Village!" Claire screamed.

I felt like shrinking into a hole. If the manager were still there, I'm sure he would have kicked us out. Lucky for us, he was gone.

Unfortunately, though, so was my Christmas spirit.

Friday

You guys are going to hate me for saying this, I just know it. But honestly, what would you do without me? Did you really think we could wait till opening day to set up everything?

Now we're ready. Monday will be fantastic. Piece of cake. One thing, though. Mallory, I'm sorry about your friends. Let's see if we can invite them to a BSC meeting. Seriously.

Just think about it. That's all.

Don't worry. Nothing bad happened to any friends of mine. Kristy was using the word "friends" loosely. She meant my "friends" at Channel 3.

It was the day after the North Pole Village escapade, and I hadn't quite recovered. The crew had scheduled another visit to our house that evening, and I wasn't really in the mood for them. So I was happy Kristy had asked all the BSC members to go to Stoneybrook Manor after our meeting.

I blew it, though. I stopped at home to drop off my book bag. Guess who was pulling up to the curb in front of my house?

My "friends."

"Hi, Mallory!" Mr. Henry called out. "I thought we wouldn't be seeing you this evening."

"You're right," I replied. "I have to go to Stoneybrook Manor."

"The old age home?" Mr. Henry asked. "Why?"

I explained about the boutique and mentioned my uncle.

"Perfect," Mr. Henry said. "What a Christmas-spirited thing to do. Not that I should be surprised, coming from a member of the Pike family. We'll be happy to drive you there."

"That's okay, it's walking distance," I said, turning up the front walkway.

"Nonsense, it's no problem at all."

Mr. Henry followed me into the house. As he chatted with my parents, I ran upstairs and dropped my books on my desk.

"I'm sure you all can use a little rest from us," I could hear him saying.

"Don't be silly," my mom replied.

"Boy, will Mal's friends be thrilled," Dad said.

"Thrilled with what?" I asked, running downstairs.

All my siblings were in the kitchen, looking kind of glum.

"With being videotaped," Mom answered. "Especially Kristy."

"You're going to *tape* us at the Manor?" I asked Mr. Henry.

"Why not?" Mr. Henry said.

"Lucky," Margo mumbled.

I wasn't expecting this. I took a deep breath. I excused myself to the bathroom and fixed my hair.

Well, you should have seen Kristy's face as the van pulled up to Stoneybrook Manor. Claudia's and Stacey's faces, for that matter, too. They were all gaping.

Kristy walked over to Mr. Henry and introduced herself. As he and the crew unpacked, she explained about the BSC and the Christmas Boutique.

I'm surprised she didn't ask him to attend a meeting.

As we walked into the Manor, Mrs. Kronauer came briskly out of the rec room. "Hello," she said, looking quizzically at Mr. Henry. "May I help you?"

When Mr. Henry told Mrs. Kronauer his plans, she nodded and shrugged. "Well, I suppose it's all right. We could use a little free publicity. As long as you don't disturb any of the residents."

"Not to worry," Mr. Henry reassured her. "We're a small crew. You won't notice us."

Mrs. Kronauer disappeared into the rec room. There, a few residents were decorating a Christmas tree and sifting through piles of donations.

Kristy, Claudia, Stacey, the crew, and I went to the kids' alcove. There, Abby and Mary Anne were putting price tags on the handmade dolls Mary Anne had brought. Jessi was hard at work, cleaning a donated high chair.

"In this area, we are collecting items of particular interest to parents and children," Kristy said to Jeannie's camera in this formal, grownup voice. "These are the members of the Baby-sitters Club, which meets conveniently on Mondays, Wednesdays, and Fridays from five-thirty to six.''

Claudia started cracking up.

"Cut," Mr. Henry said.

"What's so funny?" Kristy asked.

"You are so corny," Claudia said. "You sound like a commercial."

"What's wrong with . . ." Kristy's voice drifted off. Jeannie and Todd were now circling the room.

When they came back, Mary Anne ducked out of sight. Jessi busily tried to pull her hair into a tight bun. Abby was goofing around, trying on a baby's winter hat.

"Just be natural," Mr. Henry said. "Pretend we're not here."

Uh-huh.

I tried. I decided to help Abby. Unfortunately, she is the world's biggest ham. Before long, she had put a bib around her neck, a circular rattle around her left ear, and a pair of rubber Freddy Krueger gloves on her hands.

When she balanced a booster seat on her head, I ducked out of camera range.

I was helping Claudia put a wreath in the window when Mr. Rubin announced, "The food has arrived."

Mr. Henry's crew focused on the man as he served food behind a nearby table. "I'm Jack

Rubin," he said. "You know, I had a very good singing voice. In the service, I was in a training film . . ."

Rolls, butter, pastries, finger sandwiches, and juice cartons had been laid out. My friends and I dug in.

The residents were buzzing excitedly about the cameras.

"Is it the press?" one of them asked.

"Are they doing an exposé?" asked another.

"About time," remarked a third.

"No one told us," an elderly woman complained, giggling embarrassedly.

"She didn't put her teeth in," another woman explained to me with a mischievous grin.

Half the residents seemed annoyed, the other half curious.

Jeannie was wandering around the room, filming the preparations. Todd was still focused on Mr. Rubin, who was now singing, "Oh, what a beautiful mo-o-o-o-ornnning," way out of tune.

"Cut! Thank you, sir," Mr. Henry said, abruptly pulling Todd along to another resident. "Now, tell me, ma'am, what do you think of the young people here, helping you out?"

"Who?" the woman asked.

"Folks, let's use this back table for food," Kristy boomed out from the back of the room.

"This way, shoppers have to pass all the other items on their way. Trust me, it'll help sales."

Jeannie was now inching toward her. "Could you do that again, Kristy? And speak clearly."

"*FOLKS!*" Kristy began again.

Just then, I noticed Uncle Joe standing in the doorway, leaning against his cane.

"Hi, Uncle Joe!" I said.

"I heard you kids were coming," he said absently. "What's all this racket?"

I told him about the Old-fashioned Christmas Contest and the show. "They're interested in everything the Pike family does," I said. "They've been to our house many times. We're going to be stars!"

"Ah, is this the lucky grandfather?" Mr. Henry called out, walking toward us with Jeannie and her camera.

"Great-uncle," I corrected him.

Uncle Joe turned away. "I . . . I, uh, have to go back now."

"Heck of a job your grand-niece is doing!" Mr. Henry nudged Jeannie and said, "Catch him in the hallway."

Poor Uncle Joe. He looked so frightened and bewildered. "He really has to rest," I insisted. "You'll see him at our house on Christmas."

"Okay, cut!" Mr. Henry said. "Nice to meet you, sir." He and Jeannie ducked back into the rec room. I took Uncle Joe's arm and walked him back to his room.

I tried to chat with him, but he remained silent until he was lying on his bed. Then he said, "Sweetheart, I — I haven't been feeling very well, and you know, with the payroll taxes due . . . I don't think I'll be able to make the party."

Payroll taxes? I knew what was happening. Uncle Joe used to be an accountant, and Alzheimer's patients sometimes imagine themselves in the past.

"But Uncle Joe," I said, "I — "

"Too many people," he muttered.

He picked up the remote and turned on the TV.

I said good-bye and slumped out. Boy, did I feel awful. I shouldn't have mentioned that the Channel 3 crew was going to be at our family party. *That* was the real reason he didn't want to come.

But if I hadn't told him, then what? He would have shown up and been devastated to see them.

As I turned the corner toward the rec room, deep in thought, Mrs. Kronauer I saw walking toward me. "Hi," I began.

"Dear, I thought we agreed that the cameras would not be disruptive," she snapped. "Those people are shifting furniture around, making my custodians find extra lamps for lighting, bothering the residents. Three of them want to drop out of the boutique. We open on Monday, and I can't have this happening!"

"I — I'm so sorry!" I stammered.

"Don't get me wrong," Mrs. Kronauer went on. "I appreciate you and your friends' help, but I have asked the crew to leave, and I must now ask you not to bring them around again."

"Okay," I squeaked.

As Mrs. Kronauer walked away, I slunk back to the rec room. I felt about two feet tall.

CHAPTER 10

"O Christmas tree, O Christmas tree," Vanessa sang from the stairs, "when I chop you down, don't fall on me."

Saturday morning was snowy and cold. Outside, the sidewalk and street were blinding white in the intense sunlight. I was sipping hot cider in the kitchen, chatting with Mom. As Vanessa skipped into the kitchen, singing, I could hear my brothers and sisters running downstairs.

"It's snowing!" Claire squealed.

"You smell so nice, you look so green," Vanessa's song continued. "Excuse my axe for being mean . . ."

Mom and I cracked up.

Remember that book I told you about, *Christmas Tree Farm?* Well, guess where we Pikes were going that day.

To Quigley's Christmas Tree Nursery in Mercer, the next town over from Stoneybrook.

We were going to find the best tree, chop it down ourselves, tie it to one of the cars, and bring it home. Old-fashioned. Rugged. Just like the pioneers.

And Channel 3 would be covering our every move.

Yes, Dad had called ahead, and the nursery's owner had said the crew was welcome.

Sigh. I was not in the mood for cameras that day. Not after what had happened at Stoneybrook Manor the day before. (I'd told Mom and Dad about Uncle Joe's refusal to come for Christmas. They didn't look too happy.)

But this would be different. We'd be outside, in a wide-open space, enjoying the snow. I was determined not to let the cameras ruin our good time.

Besides, no one else in my family seemed to mind.

"They're here!" Nicky cried from the living room.

"It's showtime," said Dad as he descended the stairs.

"Rowf! Rowf!" barked Pow, scampering around him.

Ding-dong.

We met the crew at the front door. They had brought along several boxes of donuts and pastries, which we scarfed down in about five minutes. Mom served everyone hot cider, and

Nestor taped Vanessa singing her song.

"You ought to publish her songs in a book," he suggested with a laugh.

Of course, Vanessa's book was all we heard about on the drive to Quigley's.

"I'll have songs for every holiday," she said. "Christmas, Hanukkah, New Year's, Halloween — "

"What about George Washington's birthday?" Adam butted in.

"Or Veterans Day?" Jordan added.

"She could write an animal song," Claire spoke up.

Jordan groaned. "That's *veterinarian*."

In a rural area just past Stoneybrook, we turned into a driveway marked by a wooden sign saying QUIGLEY CHRISTMAS TREE NURSERY.

As I looked out the window, I smiled so hard my face hurt.

Beyond the parking lot was a huge field, filled with rows and rows of Christmas trees. Smoke was puffing from the chimney of a small shingled shack, filling the air with the smell of burning wood. Several families were already looking at trees, and I could hear laughter and happy talking. Everything was dusted with snow. Parents were pulling their kids from tree to tree on sleds.

What a place. I wished Jessi could have been

there. We'd have had no trouble being Daphne and Jezebel in nineteenth-century England.

As the Pike cars and the Channel 3 van pulled into the lot, a broad-shouldered old man stepped out of the shack and walked toward us, carrying a saw. "Welcome," he said with a smile. "I'm Andy Quigley. We're expecting you. Come on in."

Claire, Margo, Nicky, Vanessa, and the triplets darted straight for the trees. Pow dived into the snow, rolling around like crazy.

Mr. Quigley smiled at the sight. "Anyone care to come inside the hut for some cider or hot chocolate?" he asked.

"No, thanks," Mom said. "We're very full."

"Can we have an interior shot?" Mr. Henry asked. "I'd love to see Mallory taking a sip of cider, the fireplace in the background . . . Very homey, don't you think?"

"Sure," Mr. Quigley replied. "Come on in, if you can all fit. My wife's expecting you."

The truth? I was not interested in cider, hot chocolate, even water. In my stomach a blueberry jelly donut was still slugging it out with a cinnamon kruller.

I marched into the shack. Jeannie followed me, peering through the camera. A dad, mom, and toddler were inside, paying Mrs. Quigley for a tree. She was white-haired and trim, and her eyes crinkled when she smiled. Behind her a fire roared in the hearth.

The other family scooted out quickly, staring at the camera.

In the next ten minutes or so, I drank three cups of hot chocolate, put five small logs on the fire, examined a tin of maple syrup twice, and pretended to buy a wreath. Then I had to carry on the same conversation with Mrs. Quigley for four different takes. Mr. Henry thought of the words, and I said them so many times I still remember them:

Me: "Thanks for the hot chocolate."
Mrs. Quigley: "You're welcome. Nice of your family to come, Mallory. Have you picked out a tree?"
Me (looking out the window): "I think we've picked out eight of them."
(Mrs. Quigley chuckles.)

Mrs. Quigley was a great chuckler, but I was not born to be an actress. By about the third time I sounded as if I were reading a boring textbook.

In reality, my family hadn't picked out any trees yet, although Mom was examining some. Dad was pulling Nicky, Margo, and Pow on the sled.

"Faster, Rudolph, faster!" Nicky shouted.

"Neeeeiiigh!" Dad said, breaking into a run.

"Reindeers don't *neigh!*" Margo declared in a fit of giggles.

Thump! She and Nicky went flying as Dad pulled them over a bump.

They rolled into a snowbank, hooting with laughter. Pow scooted away, his stubby legs sinking into the snow.

"Did you get that?" Mr. Henry asked Todd.

"Nahh, missed it," Todd replied.

Mr. Henry turned to my dad. "Do you think we can do it over again?"

"Yeeeaaaa!" Margo and Nicky screamed.

"Us, too!" shouted a boy who was riding on another sled.

When the boy's dad shushed him and pulled him out of camera range, the boy had a fit. Mr. Henry had to stop shooting until he quieted down. By that time, Margo and Nicky had grown restless and run off. Pow was sniffing the shack.

Dad rounded up Adam and Byron. He tried to pull them over the bump, but they were too big to fall off.

We did finally manage to look for a tree. But we were never alone. It's amazing how many people are friendly to you when you're being followed by TV cameras. If I had a quarter for every kid who ran in front of a camera and waved, I'd be rich.

One family really latched on to us. A nine-year-old girl and a six-year-old boy made friends with Vanessa, Margo, and Claire. Their parents were full of advice about every single tree we looked at — which kind lasted longest, which smelled best, and so on.

The Quigley family was nice to us for the first half hour or so. But afterward they smiled less and less.

I didn't blame them. Their customers were paying more attention to us than the trees.

We ended up choosing a Norwegian fir. It was full and tall and beautiful. When Mr. Quigley started to saw it down, the three cameras swarmed around him.

"Could you move that shoulder back?" Jeannie asked.

"Let's have the triplets surrounding him," Todd said.

"How about letting them help out?" Mr. Henry suggested.

"Make sure the tree falls away from the sunlight," Nestor warned Mr. Quigley.

"Cut!" Mr. Henry said.

"That's what I'm trying to do," Mr. Quigley retorted. (I was surprised he didn't kick us all out. Or saw one of the cameras in half.)

We carried the tree to the parking lot. While Mom paid for it, Dad, the triplets, and I tied it onto the roof rack of Mom's car (as the cameras rolled, of course).

When we were done, Mr. Henry said to Jeannie, "Let's secure a camera on the rack for a point-of-view shot."

I couldn't believe it. Now they were strapping one of the cameras to the roof rack, pointing it forward so that the tree was in the shot. The camera would ride on top of the car, showing our trip home as if looking through the "eyes" of the tree.

Jordan watched them in horror. "You're breaking the branches!" he complained.

"Is this really necessary?" Dad asked Mr. Henry.

Mr. Henry exhaled loudly. "I think it would enhance the show," he said extra-patiently, like a teacher trying not to lose his temper.

"I want more cider, please," Claire announced.

"I need to go to the bathroom," Nicky declared.

"Me, too," Adam said.

"Can we buy a wreath?" Vanessa asked.

"*Just a minute!*" Dad snapped.

Pikes filed into the Quigleys' shack. Other Pikes filed into the portable bathrooms. (Pow wasn't so discreet. He made yellow snow.)

94

Still other Pikes (me) waited in the car while Mr. Henry and his crew grunted over their camera-strapping task.

We left Quigley's at about ten miles an hour (so the camera wouldn't fall). By then I'd almost forgotten about the tree.

I kind of wished the camera *would* fall. Maybe Mr. Henry would call off the shoot. I was sick and tired of it.

I couldn't wait for our old-fashioned Christmas to be over, so I could have some fun again.

CHAPTER 11

The next morning at our house, Mr. Henry said six words that really lifted my spirits:

"We'll have to leave early today."

I grinned. I nearly said, "Thank you."

It was Sunday, and the rest of the BSC members were coming over soon for our holiday party. I had told Mr. Henry about it a few days earlier, but I hadn't reminded him. And he hadn't asked.

I thought about asking him and the crew to stay, but I decided against it. I needed a break from them. We all did. The party would be much more fun without them.

In our living room, the tree was up and fully decorated. It looked gorgeous and smelled even better. The triplets' Christmas tape was playing over our speakers. I hummed along as I tidied up the room for the BSC party. Vanessa was on the couch, writing. Dad was downtown buying the newspaper, so Nicky was frantically wrapping a strange wood "sculpture" he'd hammered together for him.

Pow thought the Christmas tree stand was his own private water bowl, but I quickly steered him into the kitchen.

On the mantel of our fireplace I put the gifts I planned to give to each BSC member — eight personal journals. I'd bought eight simple blank books and decorated each one with the person's name and a collage. For Jessi, the collage contained beautiful horse pictures and ballet photos. For Kristy, sports scenes. (One problem. I'd forgotten to buy myself one. Sigh.)

Upstairs, the Channel 3 crew was filming a secret session with Margo and Mom — they were making some gift none of us was supposed to see.

Vanessa helped me put a brand-new Christmas cloth on our dining room table. Then we started setting out munchies — chips, red and green M&Ms, pretzels, brownies, chocolate-chip cookies. (Of course, a lot of them ended up in our mouths.)

Dad arrived with cold cuts and bread. He, Vanessa, and I made sandwiches, while Nicky walked around with a grin saying, "Dad, you'll never, ever, ever guess what I'm giving you for Christmas."

"That's for sure," Vanessa said under her breath.

As we were putting the sandwiches on the table, Mr. Henry and his crew came downstairs.

"Mind if we take some readings in the living room?" he asked. "We're probably going to have to relight it for tomorrow's activities."

"Relight it?" Dad said.

"Free-standing lamps, maybe a few reflectors," Mr. Henry replied with a shrug. "It's a dark room, and we want everything to look good."

"Uh-huh." Dad nodded and went back into the kitchen to get soft drinks.

Moments later, the bell rang.

I opened the door. "Merry Christmas, Happy Hanukkah, Happy Kwanzaa!" cried Kristy. As she stepped inside, holding a present, she announced in a fake English accent, "I only allow my left side to be filmed!"

I think Mr. Henry smiled, but it was hard to tell. He was busy taking light readings or something.

We exchanged presents. The rest of my family came into the room and said hi. But Kristy's eyes never left the camera crew.

"So, have you guys recovered from the filming at Stoneybrook Manor?" Kristy asked Mr. Henry.

"Oh, sure." He chuckled. "You get used to everything in this business."

"Kristy, would you like some sandwich — " I started to ask.

"I guarantee it'll be a lot easier today," she barged on.

Mr. Henry laughed. "I don't know about that. I'm going shopping with my own family in a little while."

"You mean, after the party?" Kristy asked.

Mr. Henry looked at her blankly. "What party?"

"The Baby-sitters Club party." Kristy flashed me a Look. "You know, the one Mallory's setting up for?"

"Oh, I won't be able to stay for that," Mr. Henry said.

Ding-dong.

I pulled the door open. Claudia, Mary Anne, and Abby had arrived together. We all hugged and wished each other happy holidays.

"We" did not include Kristy. She was following Mr. Henry, looking very upset.

"Well, which one of the camera people is staying?" she asked.

"Hi, Kristy!" Mary Anne said, handing her a present.

"Hi. Thanks. Just a second." Kristy turned back to Mr. Henry.

He shrugged. "I'm afraid we planned the

day off. We need a holiday break, too."

"But you can't do this!" Kristy blurted out.

I tugged on Claudia's sleeve. "Merry Christmas!" she exclaimed, pulling Kristy away. "I have the coolest present to give you."

"But I — they — " Kristy sputtered.

Mr. Henry had disappeared into the kitchen. Claudia, Mary Anne, Abby, and I practically dragged Kristy to the dining room table, where my brothers and sisters were wolfing down sandwiches (enviously watched by Pow).

"Mallory, why are you letting them go?" Kristy asked in a loud whisper.

"She can't tell them what to do," Abby said.

"But this was the best part of the film," Kristy went on.

As Mr. Henry walked back through the dining room, he called out, "Have a great party, kids! See you in a few days!"

We weren't fast enough to hold Kristy back. "Mr. Henry, you look like a guy who could use a good baby-sitter," she said. "We're running a special deal, two nights free sitting for every ten minutes of filming — "

Mr. Henry laughed. "You sure are persistent, but I'm not — "

"Three nights for five minutes!" Kristy shot back.

"My kids are twenty-one and twenty-five," Mr. Henry said.

"Oh."

Kristy slumped back to the table. To a loud chorus of good-byes, the camera crew left.

"It's okay, Kristy," I said. "Really. They can be a pain."

"No pain, no gain." Glowering, Kristy plopped in a chair and picked up a sandwich.

"You'll get your chance for fame and fortune," Abby reassured her.

Kristy took a bite and chewed. "All I woofa wah leo pubbissy."

"My thoughts exactly," Claudia said.

We all giggled, except Kristy. She swallowed and said, "All I wanted was a little publicity. *Someone* has to be thinking about that."

She said that last part glaring at me.

Fortunately the bell rang again. One by one, the other BSC members arrived.

We opened our presents. Everyone loved the journals. We turned up the Christmas carols. We played a CD of Hanukkah songs that Abby had brought, as well as Jessi's Kwanzaa music. We ate like pigs and laughed a lot.

It would have been a great party if Kristy hadn't looked like the ghost of Jacob Marley.

CHAPTER 12

Monday

After today, I think we ought to give some serious thought to changing our name. I mean, maybe it's time to move on. We've baby-sat for a long time. We've been through tantrums and sicknesses and strange feeding schedules and boo-boos and diapers.

How does the name Elder—sitters Club sound?

Stacey wasn't really looking forward to the opening night of the Christmas Boutique. Her boyfriend, Robert, and his family had invited her to go a concert in Stamford. But she had told them no.

No one would have minded if she'd gone to the concert. Both associate members, Shannon and Logan, had agreed to help out at the Manor, so we had plenty of people.

I think Stacey was worried about the Wrath of Thomas. You see, when Stace first started going out with Robert, she began missing meetings, being late, and switching jobs on short notice — so Kristy kicked her out. (Well, Stacey also quit at the same time. I don't remember which came first.) Later they worked things out and Stacey rejoined. But ever since then, she's been on her absolute best behavior.

I could tell she wasn't in the greatest mood on Monday. She was scowling when she met Claudia and me on the corner of Elm Street and Burnt Hill Road. The boutique was going to open at five o'clock, but we were supposed to be there half an hour early to set up. (Our meeting had been canceled, so Claudia's answering machine was taking messages.) Claudia and I were carrying our donations. Mine was a plastic bag full of spare decorations my family had made. Claudia's was a wrapped-up painting in one hand and a shopping bag full of books. (Her mom's a librarian and had agreed to donate books the library didn't need.)

"Hi, Stace," Claud and I said.

"Rrrmf," Stacey replied (approximately). "What's in the bag?"

"Library books," Claud said. "Overstocks, Mom calls them."

"Uh-huh."

We began walking. We switched off carrying Claudia's heavy bag. Stacey didn't say much. She was still thinking about the concert she was missing.

The Manor was really jumping when we got there. Abby, Kristy, Shannon, and Jessi were already bustling about. Someone had set up a stereo system in the rec room, and it was loudly playing the kind of music you hear in old movies. Some of the old folks were dancing as they set up the tables. A balding guy with a huge belly was trying to do the jitterbug with Kristy.

Stacey laughed out loud. (Her bad mood couldn't survive that sight.)

Abby and Jessi greeted us. "Hey, more donations! Thanks!" Jessi said. "Bring the books over to Mrs. Blanchard."

She led us to the book table. Mrs. Blanchard

was an elderly woman busily arranging the books by topic.

Jessi introduced us and Stacey handed over the bag. Mrs. Blanchard pulled out three books and read the titles: *"Elementary Thermodynamics, The Social Structure of Arachnids, Seismology and Tectonic Science . . ."* She laughed. "Hm, real best-sellers."

"Maybe we can give them away as bonuses," Stacey suggested.

"They'd make great doorstops," Claudia said.

"Booster seats," I added.

Mrs. Blanchard laughed. "Well, we do have a bargain pile." She opened up the top book and wrote 10¢.

I stayed to give her a hand. Stacey and Kristy moved on to the kids' alcove. They helped Abby, who was sorting several piles of newly donated clothes and putting them into labeled cardboard boxes on the table. Next to the boxes was a gorgeous display of decorated frames, collages, and origami that Jessi had brought.

"When Mary Anne and Logan show up, they'll stay here with Abby," Kristy said to Stacey. "Jessi and Claudia will help out with the books. Mallory and I will move to the nursery to help Shannon. You're in charge of taking kids to and from the nursery. Okay?"

"Uh-huh."

Kristy folded some onesies and put them into the BOY-INFANT box. "So," she said, "is Robert coming?"

"No," Stacey said through gritted teeth. "He's at a concert with his parents."

Kristy nodded. "Sounds fun. Too bad they didn't invite you, huh?"

Before Stacey could scream, Claudia swept by with two plates, one with brownies and the other with warm bread. "Anybody hungry? These are homemade by Mr. Rubin, the guy in charge of the food table. The bread is sugar-free. Mr. Rubin said so. He's diabetic, too."

"Thanks!" Kristy said, grabbing a brownie.

Taking a piece of bread, Stacey glanced at the food table. Mr. Rubin smiled and gave her a thumbs-up.

Mrs. Kronauer walked into the room, holding a megaphone. "Attention, please, ladies and gentlemen!" she called out. "I can see we're off to a fantastic start. We have more donations than we could possibly have expected."

A happy murmur went up from the room.

"Before the crowds arrive," Mrs. Kronauer continued, "I'd like to give a special thanks to the young people you see around you. I don't know what we would have done without the

106

help of the girls of the Baby-sitters Club!"

The residents cheered. At that moment, Mary Anne and Logan arrived. Kristy pointed to Logan and shouted, "A boy, too!"

Logan's face turned the color of cherry Kool-Aid.

Mrs. Kronauer nodded politely and continued. "I'm told by Kristy that we have a special entertainment treat in store around six o'clock. So without further ado, back to work!"

"What's the treat?" Stacey asked Kristy.

"You'll see," Kristy replied.

Mary Anne and Logan went to the kids' alcove. As Stacey and Abby explained what to do, Kristy and I ran to the nursery.

Shortly after five, the boutique had its first customers, the Barrett/DeWitt family. They're almost as large as the Pike family — seven kids, from two previous marriages. Mrs. DeWitt's are named Buddy (eight years old), Suzi (five), and Marnie (two). Mr. DeWitt's are Lindsay (eight), Taylor (six), Madeline (four), and Ryan (two).

"Toys!" Suzi squealed, making a beeline for the kids' section. Lindsay and Taylor scampered after her.

"How would the rest of you like to go to the playroom?" Stacey asked. She smiled at Marnie and Ryan, who were clutching their parents' hands.

"Yeeeeah!" the toddlers replied.

"Sounds terrific," Mrs. DeWitt said.

"Is there stuff for big kids?" Buddy asked. "This place is boring."

"Yeah, this place is boring," Madeline echoed.

"You're just copying me," Buddy complained.

"Am not."

"Come on, guys," Stacey said. She led the kids out of the room, down the hallway, and into the nursery. Kristy, Shannon, and I were there, busily laying out some snacks Mrs. Kronauer had brought in.

The kids shoveled in some junk food. Marnie then began riding around on a toy truck. Ryan and Madeline played trains on a Brio track. Buddy attacked a jigsaw puzzle.

Stacey was like a shuttle train. Every few seconds she dropped off or picked up another kid. First Mathew and Johnny Hobart arrived, then Jenny Prezzioso, then Laurel and Patsy Kuhn.

When Stacey brought in Nina Marshall, she crinkled her nose.

"What's wrong?" I asked.

My sense of smell immediately answered the question. That, and the concentrated look on Ryan DeWitt's face.

"Guess what we don't have?" Kristy asked.

"Uh-oh," Shannon murmured.

"Mrs. DeWitt has a diaper bag," Stacey said. "I'll get it."

I opened a window.

Stacey ran into the boutique and found Mrs. DeWitt, who apologized for not giving her the bag in the first place.

In a moment, the crisis was solved.

Ryan was only her first diaper change of the evening. Altogether we had to do four.

Before long, the boutique was wall-to-wall people. Abby, Mary Anne, and Logan had their hands full in the kids' alcove. Parents and kids were pawing through the boxes, strewing stuff everywhere. Jessi and Claudia were also busy at the book table. After a while, Charlotte Johanssen began helping Stacey shuttle the kids. (She's an eight-year-old BSC charge who's very close to Stacey.)

Ben Hobart, my boyfriend (kind of), had stopped by the nursery. He and I listened while Kristy explained her secret plan: "Mr. Rubin knows how to play the piano, so I asked him if he'd play carols for the kids. Like a singalong. He loved the idea." Then she called out, "Who wants to sing carols?"

"Meeeeee!" Hands flew up into the air.

"Great," Kristy said. "Stacey and I will round up the kids who are in the other room. We'll start at six o'clock sharp."

She and Stacey ran into the boutique.

The rest of us gathered up the little kids and followed.

As we entered the boutique, I looked around for Uncle Joe. He was nowhere to be seen.

"Can you take over for me a minute while I find Uncle Joe?" I asked Ben.

"Sure," he replied.

I ran to my great-uncle's room. He was lying in bed, staring out the window. A magazine was open on his chest.

"Hi, Uncle Joe!" I said. "Why aren't you at the boutique?"

He looked at me crossly for a moment. Then his expression softened. "Visiting hours already?" he asked.

I patiently explained about the boutique. He nodded, as if he were hearing about it for the first time. "Well, I'll go," he said, "if you promise to be my bodyguard."

"You bet." He stood up and I took his arm. Together we walked down the hall.

Stacey was gathering kids by the piano when we entered. Among the singers were Jordan, Nicky, Vanessa, Margo, and Claire.

"Jingle bells, jingle bells, jingle all the way . . ."

The place fell silent and listened. You should have seen the looks on those kids' faces. Even

Adam Pike, the Terror of Slate Street, looked angelic.

I felt so wonderful I almost cried. Part of it was because I was with Uncle Joe. Part of it was because the boutique was such a big success.

You know what else? Not one TV camera was in sight.

That, I think, was the best part of all.

In a funny way, I felt that the Christmas season had just begun.

As for Stacey? Well, she said she cried during the singing. And she didn't regret missing the concert with Robert's family, not for one minute.

CHAPTER 13

Here is the number one best thing about a Pike family Christmas: Secret Santas.

Do you have that tradition with your family? You should. It's so much fun. Everyone writes a wish on a strip of paper and tosses the paper into a hat. Then someone mixes the papers up, and everyone picks one.

Your job, as a "Secret Santa," is to grant the wish you have picked. You're allowed to be as creative as you want (and you have to be, if the wish is really weird). A sense of humor helps, too.

We'd made our selections the day after the Christmas Boutique opening. I made my own wish pretty easy. I wrote, *I wish for the greatest Christmas book of all time*. I figured someone would buy me Dickens's *A Christmas Carol* or something else wonderful.

Whose wish did I pick? Adam's:

I would like an iguana or a snake or a gila monster. Or all.

No sweat. At a toy store I bought him a disgusting, realistic, slimy python. I knew he'd love it.

I couldn't wait for Christmas Eve. That's when we exchange Secret Santa presents.

The days before Christmas Eve are a big blur now. I remember a lot of baking. And shopping. And helping Mom and Margo knit a cap for Dad. And more shopping. And some door-to-door Christmas caroling. And more shopping.

But most of all, I remember little round camera lenses staring at me.

Well, all except for two afternoons, Tuesday and Thursday, when I helped out at the Stoneybrook Manor Christmas Boutique. Boy, was I glad the Channel 3 crew had been kicked out of there. I felt much more relaxed without them.

On Christmas Eve morning, our doorbell rang at 8:11. I know, because my eyes went right to my clock when they opened.

Apparently no one else was awake either, because the bell rang again. I stumbled out of bed and walked toward my door.

"Just a minute!" I heard Dad call out.

When I reached the top of the stairs, I could hear Dad opening the front door and saying, "Couldn't you guys make it a little later? No one's awake."

"Sorry," Mr. Henry's voice answered. "We'll be silent. We have a lot of extra equipment, and it's going to take awhile to set up. Look at it this way: since we're setting up today, we can let you sleep later tomorrow morning."

How nice of them.

"All right," rumbled Dad. "Anyone want coffee?"

"Decaf, if you have it," I heard Jeannie say.

Poor Dad. I ducked back into my room and dressed. By the time I went downstairs, Margo, Vanessa, and Nicky were in the kitchen. They were still in their pajamas, and Dad was pouring cereal.

We all said good morning and not much else. I helped Dad. Pow waddled in sleepily and lapped at his bowl.

A minute later Mom came downstairs. She looked dazed.

" 'Morning," Dad said. "Do we have decaf?"

Mom shook her head. "Put it on the list. Along with brown sugar, salsa, some extra chocolate chips, and the deli stuff."

"What deli stuff?" Dad asked.

"For sandwiches," Mom said. "To have when the neighbors drop by."

"Neighbors?" Dad said.

Mom took a deep breath. "Yes. You know, people who live on our block. Who always seem to drop by on Christmas Eve to chat. And who will most certainly do so this year in great numbers when they see that TV cameras are here."

"Okay, dear, I'll run out and — "

"No, never mind, I can use the fresh air."

With that, Mom stormed out.

Chew, chew, chew. We all chewed silently.

Dad tried to look cheerful as the rest of my brothers and sisters filed in.

Crash!

I jumped at the noise from the living room. Pow ran in, growling. A moment later, Nestor ran into the kitchen, asking, "Do you have a broom? We busted a lightbulb."

Dad walked out with him to the broom closet. The rest of us quietly finished breakfast.

Mom returned a short while later with the groceries. In the meantime, Todd had driven to a nearby deli for cups of coffee.

"Fresh hazelnut-flavored coffee for everyone!" Mom sang cheerily as she walked through the front door.

"No, thanks, we're fine," Mr. Henry said.

Mom's smile disappeared. "Who's going to help in the kitchen?" she called out, trying to sound normal.

"Me!" shouted Vanessa, Byron, Nicky, and I.

We followed her to the kitchen. We unpacked groceries. Vanessa and I started making sandwiches. Byron and Nicky helped Mom set out the ingredients for chocolate-chip cookies.

Mr. Henry peeked into the kitchen. "Can we borrow some paper towels?"

"Right over there." Mom pointed to the rack under the cupboard.

Mr. Henry took the whole roll. "Thanks. Be right back."

"Okay, Nicky," Mom said, "break the egg carefully — "

Splat!

"Ewww!" Vanessa cried, jumping away. "He got it on my feet!"

I reached for the paper towels.

No paper towels.

"Ew! Ew! Ew! Ew!" Vanessa repeated.

I ran into the living room. I saw a wad of paper towels soaking up a coffee stain on a windowsill. The rest of the roll, covered with dirty handprints, was on the floor.

I grabbed it and ran back to the kitchen.

Pow was licking Vanessa's feet. She and I pushed him away and cleaned off the rest of the egg.

Adam and Jordan wandered in and started eating chocolate chips. Mom yelled at them. Claire and Margo started fighting in the den. Dad yelled at them. Something thumped in the living room. Mr. Henry yelled at Nestor.

Ding-dong.

"I'll get it!" screamed about six voices.

I ran for the door. Unfortunately I hadn't noticed the wires lying across the floor.

I took a tumble my gym teacher would have been proud of.

"You okay?" Mr. Henry asked.

"Merry Christmas!" shouted Mr. and Mrs. Arnold, pushing open the half-closed door.

I sprang to my feet. Mom and Dad were tiptoeing around the wires. "Hi!" Mom called out. "Come on in!"

(She sounded worried about that last part.)

"Nicky dropped the sandwiches in the sink!" Vanessa yelled from the kitchen.

"Excuse me," Dad said, bolting away.

Mom and I tried valiantly to carry on a normal conversation with Mr. and Mrs. Arnold and Marilyn and Carolyn. We couldn't sit, because the sofa and chairs were full of camera equipment. And the crew was running around like crazy. I must have heard "Excuse me" a million times.

Soon the smell of burning cookies wafted into the living room. "We forgot to set the timer!" Nicky called out.

"Be right back!" Mom said.

What a nightmare. One batch of cookies was charcoal.

Eventually we managed to salvage four decent sheets of cookies. And only one sandwich had been destroyed by Nicky's carelessness.

Mom had been right. The whole neighborhood did show up at the house. (Very well dressed, too.) Dad made the crew take their junk off our furniture so we could sit down.

Finally, around one o'clock, the visitors left.

"Okay, let's do Secret Santas now, or forever hold our peace!" Dad announced.

We gathered in the living room. The crew had finished setting up, and the place actually looked sort of neat. Dad plugged in the Christmas tree lights. Adam put the triplets' cassette tape on. Mom brought in a tray full of piping hot drinks — hazelnut coffee for her and Dad, hot chocolate for the rest of us.

Dad stood by the tree. All of our presents were under it. I'd wrapped Adam's snake in a huge box to fake him out. I could see him eyeing it curiously.

Closing his eyes, Dad said, "I will pick, totally at random, the very first gift from a Secret — "

"Uh, excuse me, we're not rolling," Mr. Henry interrupted, waving Jeannie over.

"Come on!" Jordan complained.

"Action!" Mr. Henry said.

Dad reached under the tree.

"Cut!" Mr. Henry said. "Say the intro again, will you? Okay, action."

Dad repeated the part about picking at random. Then he reached under the tree and took out a long box. He looked at the tag and read, "For Vanessa!"

"Yeeeaaa!" Vanessa screamed. She grabbed the box and said, "My wish was to become rich and famous."

She tore it open. Inside was a stack of fake hundred-dollar bills and a newspaper with a huge banner headline:

VANESSA PIKE ELECTED PRESIDENT!!!

Vanessa clutched the money and burst out laughing. "Ya-hooo! My wish came true!"

"I got her that at the mall," Adam bragged.

"Cut!" Mr. Henry said. "Let's get a close-up of that headline. Okay . . . action."

Dad patiently let Jeannie zoom in on the newspaper.

"Cut!" Mr. Henry called out. "Okay, long shot. . . . Okay, Mr. Pike . . . action!"

Dad reached under the tree and picked another. "This is for — "

"Cut!" Mr. Henry yelled.

"NO-O-O-O-O!"

Byron's scream nearly made me lose my hearing.

"No! No! No! No! No! No!" Byron was on his feet now, stamping around the living room. "No cutting! I'm sick of cutting!"

"Shh, shhh," Mom said, "it's all right." She stood up and put her arm gently around his shoulder.

"That's my box!" Byron whined. "I looked."

"Okay, calm down." As Mom led him back to the couch, she glared at Mr. Henry. "Can we roll now?"

"Action," he said with an apologetic shrug.

"This one belongs to . . . Byron!" Dad announced.

"I wished for my own phone," Byron said.

Inside his box was an ancient, battered old Fisher-Price telephone that Claire used to play with.

Byron howled. He picked up the receiver and said, "Send over twenty-seven pizzas — now!"

Dad squatted down to reach under the tree again.

Ffffft! A lightbulb on one of the crew's lamps burned out.

"Cut!" Mr. Henry said.

"Ohhhhhhhh!" Vanessa groaned.

"This is *boring!*" Adam said.

"I hate this Christmas!" Jordan shouted. "Why do we have to have these stupid cameras around?"

"Make them leave," Margo said. "Please, Dad? Mom?"

Mom looked as if she were about to cry. Dad looked furious. I expected him to chew all of us out. I hoped he wouldn't be on camera while he did it.

Dad stood up and took a deep breath. He turned to Mr. Henry. "Would you please leave?"

Huh? For a moment I wasn't sure who he was talking to.

Mr. Henry looked as if he'd been asked to stand on his head and sing "The Star-Spangled Banner."

"Excuse me?" he asked.

"Just for a couple of hours," Dad said. "We need a little break, okay?"

"Sure," Mr. Henry said with an uncertain nod. "We'll take a lunch break."

We waited quietly while they set down their stuff and left.

"Now," Dad said. "Let's do this the way it's meant to be done."

Yea, Dad!

He handed out all the gifts, without interruption. Adam loved his gross snake. He chased Claire around the living room with it.

You know what my gift was? My "greatest Christmas book of all time"?

A blank journal, bought for me by Vanessa, with the inscription: *It hasn't been written yet. Get to work.*

It was the most wonderful gift I could have hoped for. I gave her a huge hug and kiss.

"Dad," Nicky asked timidly, "do we have to let the camera crew come back?"

"Say no, say no, say no," pleaded Vanessa, the Old-fashioned Christmas Contest winner, the one who got us into this mess in the first place.

Dad sighed and looked at Mom.

"I think," Mom said, "it's time for a family meeting."

CHAPTER 14

We cleared the dining room table. Then we brought our mugs to the kitchen to be refilled with hot chocolate.

The mugs steamed as we set them down on the table for our meeting. To me, the table looked like a small English village of houses with smoking chimneys.

I guess I still had my mind on the idea of an old-fashioned Christmas season. December had started out that way, but it sure had changed. It had gone from old-fashioned to out-of-control.

"So, guys, what are we going to do?" Dad asked.

"Ssssstrike fasssssst and sssstrike deep," Adam said, moving his snake closer to Claire.

"Sto-o-o-op!" Claire protested.

"Adam, put that away," Mom demanded. "Before Mr. Henry comes back, we need to have a serious discussion."

"I am sssseriousss," Adam said. "We should buy real sssnakessss and hide them in the camera equipment."

"Or maybe rats," Byron suggested.

"Ew, gross," Margo said.

"Porcupines!" Claire piped up.

"The cameraman asked us to pose," Vanessa recited, "when a snake popped out and bit him on the nose!"

Dad was laughing. "Uh, do I sense that we're all a little tired of the TV crew?"

So many heads nodded, it looked as if a small earthquake were shaking the room.

"They get in the way," Adam said.

"They break stuff," Margo added.

"They almost messed up the Stoneybrook Manor Christmas Boutique," I said.

Mom nodded. "And they scared Uncle Joe away from our party."

"They made the man yell at North Pole Village," Claire chimed in.

"They stepped on Pow," Vanessa grumbled.

I sighed. "I wanted us to have this great Christmas, just like the olden days. But it hasn't been any fun at all."

There. I had said it as plainly as I could.

"I know what you mean," Mom said. "It was kind of exciting at first."

"And we're rich," Jordan added.

"So?" Adam snapped. "It doesn't feel any different."

Byron was pouting. "Tomorrow's going to be so stupid. Merry Christmas — cut! Pass the turkey — cut! Deck the halls with cut-cut-cut!"

"Silent cu-u-ut," Margo sang. "Ho-o-oly cu-u-ut!"

"It doesn't have to be that awful," Dad said. "We could tell them to leave."

"We did already," Nicky spoke up.

Dad shook his head. "I mean for good. Kick them out."

"We can't," I reminded him. "You signed a contract. They paid us all that money."

"A contract is an exchange," Mom said. "We can cancel it at any time, if we give them back what they gave us. Dad made sure to write that into the contract."

"Give back ten thousand dollars?" Jordan asked.

"We were doing okay without it," Dad replied. "If we gave it back, we wouldn't be any different than we were last month."

"Yeah, we would," Byron mumbled. "We'd be happy."

For a moment, no one said a word. I looked at Vanessa. She'd been pretty quiet, sitting back in her chair and twiddling the ends of her hair.

She tilted her head lower, so that her hair fell in front of her face. When she spoke, her voice was barely audible. "I'm sorry."

"For what?" Mom asked.

"For entering that dumb contest," Vanessa replied.

Mom leaned over and put an arm around her. "It's not your fault, sweetheart. You meant well, and we're all proud of you. No one could have predicted how this would end up."

Vanessa began sniffling.

"Maybe we should put this to a vote," Dad suggested. "All those in favor of banishing Channel Three, raise your hands."

My hand shot up. So did Byron's, Adam's, Margo's, Claire's, and Nicky's. Then Mom's and Dad's. Vanessa wiped her eyes on a napkin and raised her arm, too.

Jordan sat there with his arms folded. He scowled and mumbled something about not being rich anymore.

Then, reluctantly, he raised his hand, too.

When the doorbell rang, we had just finished cleaning up. As Mom and Dad opened the door, we all gathered behind them.

"Hi, there!" Mr. Henry said. "Everyone well rested and ready?"

126

He walked past my parents, taking off his gloves and hat. Nestor, Jeannie, and Todd trudged in behind him, clutching paper cups.

I looked at Dad. He was glancing at Mom.

He's chickening out! I thought.

"Okay, let's use that higher wattage bulb, Todd," Mr. Henry said, then turned toward Dad. "Does the house have fuses or circuit breakers?"

Dad swallowed. Then he said, "Mr. Henry, I'm afraid there's been a change of plans."

Mr. Henry cocked his head impatiently.

"You see," Dad went on. "We're kicking you out."

Mr. Henry burst out laughing. So did Nestor. Jeannie and Todd ignored the remark.

"I know, I know, what a morning, huh?" Mr. Henry barged on. "The reason I ask is because we're adding some equipment that may be a drain on the current, so — "

"I'm serious," Dad said firmly. "We'd like to stop shooting. For good."

Now all three camera people turned around. No one was laughing.

"Well, that's not possible," Mr. Henry said. "I mean, I know it's been a little stressful this morning — "

"It's not just this morning," Mom spoke up. "This whole process has worn us down, Mr.

Henry. We would like a real, family Christmas. By ourselves. Not fancied up and edited and posed for TV viewers."

Mr. Henry smiled nervously. "Look, we're all tired. Our tempers are short. The kids are restless. Don't you worry. We've got a lot of terrific footage already, and I know the show will be a huge success. But without Christmas Eve and Christmas, we have no show. Everything goes to waste. The film, the work, the salaries — "

"Well, I'm sure ten thousand dollars would go a long way to pay for the loss," Dad said.

Mom scooted into the kitchen and returned with a checkbook.

"Please," Mr. Henry said. "Let's not be rash about this."

"He has a rash?" Claire whispered to me.

"Ssshhh," I said.

Mom was already writing out a check.

"Nothing rash at all," Dad said. "I appreciate your efforts, Mr. Henry. I know how hard you've worked. But the truth is, what you're filming is simply a lie. How many wholesome, all-American Christmases involve cutting, reshooting, and staging? Not to mention interrupted sleep and big arguments in public places."

"But that — we agreed — " Mr. Henry sputtered.

"If you want an example of how a family operates together, here it is," Mom said, handing Mr. Henry the check. "By unanimous decision at a Pike family meeting, we have decided to cancel our contract and return your money."

Mr. Henry's face turned bright red. He glared at the check as if he wanted to burn it with his eyesight. I thought he was going to explode.

Claire grasped my hand tightly.

Then, with a curt nod, Mr. Henry took the check and stuffed it in his pocket. "Your choice," he said sharply. "Okay, crew, let's wrap."

Without another word, the three camera people began collecting their equipment.

My family and I moved into the kitchen. Out of the crew's sight, Claire and Margo started jumping with excitement. The triplets and Nicky leaped as high as they could to smack high fives. Even Pow looked happy. Dad and Mom hugged. I could hear Mom whisper, "I'm so relieved."

She'd taken the words right out of my mouth.

"Mallory," Dad said softly, "give Uncle Joe a try on the phone. Tell him what happened. Maybe he'll change his mind about tomorrow."

I sat by the kitchen phone and tapped out the Stoneybrook Manor number. The switchboard put me through to Uncle Joe's room.

After about ten rings, I heard, "Yes?"

"Uncle Joe, it's Mallory!"

"Hello, dear, what can I do you for?"

I patiently explained that the camera crew was gone for good. "It'll just be us for Christmas, Uncle Joe. No one else. Please join us. You'll have such a good time, and we're dying to see you."

"I don't know. My back isn't what it used to be — "

"Dad'll pick you up," I said.

"Well, of course he will. He wouldn't expect me to walk!"

"So you'll come?" I asked.

Claire and Margo started jumping up and down again.

Uncle Joe sighed. "I guess the alternative is spending it with Connor. I'm not willing to suffer that much. Okay, tell your dad I'll be in the lobby at ten o'clock sharp. If he's not there, I'm heading back to bed."

Now *that* sounded like Uncle Joe. "Great! I'll tell him," I said. "Thanks. I love you."

"Me, too," Uncle Joe said with a chuckle.

I said good-bye, hung up, and let out a scream. "He said yes!"

"Yeeeeea!" my sibs cheered.

In the living room, the crew was unloading the last of the equipment. Jeannie ducked into the kitchen and smiled. "You made the right decision," she whispered. "Merry Christmas."

"Merry Christmas," we whispered back.

She bustled out the front door. The living room fell silent. We heard the rumble of the van outside.

"Well," Dad said, "what are we waiting for? I think some presents need to be put under the tree — it's Christmas Eve!"

I'm sure Mr. Henry heard our howl of delight, even if he was a block away.

CHAPTER 15

*T*hump *thump thump thump thump thump thump thump!* "Eeeeeeeeee!"

No, it wasn't a herd of screaming wildebeests. (Do wildebeests scream?) It was the sound of the Pike family Christmas morning assault.

That's about the only way to describe it — eight kids and a dog storming downstairs and diving under the tree at the same time.

And we didn't have to trip over any wires. Or stop. Or do it over.

"Cut!" Dad called from the top of the stairs.

"No way!" Byron yelled happily.

"Get out of here!" Vanessa called.

"Nyah-nyah-nyah-nyah-nyah," Claire sang.

Dad and Mom held hands as they walked downstairs. "Feels good, doesn't it?" Dad said.

As we collected our piles of presents, Claire cried out, "Look! Santa ate the cookies!"

Margo raised an eyebrow. "Claire . . ."

"Well, they're gone!" Claire insisted. "And so's the milk, and the celery for the reindeer!"

Margo looked at Mom. Mom gave her a wink, as if to say, *Our little secret*.

I loved my presents. Mom had knitted me the thickest, softest scarf. Vanessa had written a book of poems for me. The triplets and Nicky had made me (and everyone else) some homemade chocolates. (I have no idea when they were able to do it.)

I made sure Dad and I left for Stoneybrook Manor on time. He wore the hat Margo and I had knitted for him, which looked a little lopsided.

When we arrived, Uncle Joe was not in the lobby. He and Mr. Connor were in their room, playing cards.

We gently reminded Uncle Joe about the time, then helped him out to the car. He grumbled during the drive home. He complained as we walked him to the front door of our house.

The moment we stepped onto the porch, the door flew open. "Hiiiii!" shouted my brothers and sisters.

They surrounded Uncle Joe, gabbing and kissing him and showing off presents. Vanessa and the triplets had pasted a photo of Uncle Joe on a sheet of white cardboard and written

WE LOVE YOU, UNCLE JOE! around it.

I was worried about all the commotion. I thought Uncle Joe would be scared and demand to be taken back.

But all he said was, "Thank you. Let me sit on the couch, please."

A tear was slowly making its way down his stubbly left cheek.

I have never seen Uncle Joe so happy. Or looking so strong. He even helped pump up this humongous green exercise ball that Mom and Dad had given Claire.

We ate. We drank. We played. We listened to music. We played some more. Vanessa read aloud parts of my Christmas story, which I had finished and given to her. Then we ate and drank and played again. Dad took lots of photos.

That was it. All day long. Simple. Relaxed. Absolutely perfect.

Around two-thirty, Dad drove Uncle Joe back to the Manor. After such a wonderful day, did Uncle Joe bid us some emotional farewell? Some deep, tearful message of thanks?

The last thing he said as he walked out the door with Dad was, "Send me some of those photos, will you, so I can plaster them all over my room. That kind of thing drives Connor crazy."

I guess that was his way of saying he'd had a good time.

A few minutes after they left, we heard "We Wish You a Merry Christmas" being sung on the porch.

I pulled the door open. The other BSC members were standing there, warbling away.

"And a happy Hanukkahhhhhh . . . and Kwanzaaaaa . . . and New Yeeeeeear!" they ended the song.

They hustled into the house. Hugs, kisses, and "happy holidays" galore. My brothers and sisters surrounded them, brandishing their presents all over again.

"To what do we owe this great surprise?" Mom asked.

Kristy shrugged. "I felt kind of bad about the BSC party. You know, the way I complained when the TV crew left? So I called everybody and asked if they wanted to stop by."

"*Asked?*" Claudia said.

" 'Be at Slate and Burnt Hill,' " Abby imitated Kristy. " 'Two forty-five, sharp!' "

Kristy was turning pink. "I wasn't that bad . . ."

It was great to see them. The timing was perfect, too. I'm not sure Uncle Joe would have appreciated the company.

My friends stayed for only about a half hour of eating, gabbing, and oohing and ahhing at presents. They left when Kristy's brother arrived to pick her up.

Afterward Mom said, "It sure is nice to have a *welcome* interruption."

I knew what she meant. What a difference the last day had been, without the cameras.

Sure, we had given up our chance to be stars. And we had thrown ten thousand dollars out the window. But for that money, we had sacrificed a lot. Now it felt as if we'd finally reclaimed our lives. And just in time.

That night, we sang carols around the fire. I fell asleep and Dad had to carry me up to bed. It was the first time that had happened in years.

And I think it was the best night of sleep I ever had.

Dear Reader:

As a kid, Christmas was always my favorite holiday, and now as an adult it still is. In fact, I usually take the entire month of December off just to prepare for the holiday. I buy presents for my friends and relatives, I sew Christmas and Hanukkah outfits for my godchildren, and I always give a big party. All my friends and their children come to it. Every year the kids work on special art projects. It can get pretty messy. Maybe I should hire a baby-sitter to help out!

Nothing like what happened in *Mallory's Christmas Wish* has ever happened to me, but an old-fashioned Christmas is something I always wish for. I guess I'm old-fashioned at heart.

Happy reading!

Ann M. Martin

P.S. Hodges Soileau, the artist for all the covers of the Baby-sitters Club books, finally posed for one of his own paintings. Look on the front — he's the man in the green jacket.

Ann M. Martin

About the Author

ANN MATTHEWS MARTIN was born on August 12, 1955. She grew up in Princeton, NJ, with her parents and her younger sister, Jane.

Although Ann used to be a teacher and then an editor of children's books, she's now a full-time writer. She gets the ideas for her books from many different places. Some are based on personal experiences. Others are based on childhood memories and feelings. Many are written about contemporary problems or events.

All of Ann's characters, even the members of the Baby-sitters Club, are made up. (So is Stoneybrook.) But many of her characters are based on real people. Sometimes Ann names her characters after people she knows, other times she chooses names she likes.

In addition to the Baby-sitters Club books, Ann Martin has written many other books for children. Her favorite is *Ten Kids, No Pets* because she loves big families and she loves animals. Her favorite Baby-sitters Club book is *Kristy's Big Day*. (By the way, Kristy is her favorite baby-sitter!)

Ann M. Martin now lives in New York with her cats, Gussie and Woody. Her hobbies are reading, sewing, and needlework — especially making clothes for children.

Notebook Pages

This Baby-sitters Club book belongs to _____ .

I am _____ years old and in the _____ grade.

The name of my school is _____ .

I got this BSC book from _____ .

I started reading it on _____ and

finished reading it on _____ .

The place where I read most of this book is _____ .

My favorite part was when _____ .

If I could change anything in the story, it might be the part when

_____

My favorite character in the Baby-sitters Club is _____ .

The BSC member I am most like is _____

because _____ .

If I could write a Baby-sitters Club book it would be about ____

_____

_____ .

#92 Mallory's Christmas Wish

Mallory's big holiday wish is to have a nice, traditional Christmas with her family. The last big holiday wish I made was _____. This is what happened after I made the wish: _____. If I could wish for anything in the world right now, it would be for _____ _____.

Mallory is happy because in the end her wish comes true. The best wish I ever had that came true was _____ _____. One wish that still hasn't come true is _____.

As a result of Mallory's wish, her family ends up on TV. If my family were on TV, they would have to call the show _____ _____. If there was a camera crew in my house for the holidays, the silliest thing they would see would be _____.

The best thing they would see would be _____.
My favorite holiday is _____ because _____. My least favorite holiday is _____ because _____

MALLORY'S

Age 2 —
Already
a fan of
reading

Age 10 —
Still a fan.
Waiting to
meet my
favorite
author.

SCRAPBOOK

Two of my favorite things—babysitting and Ben.

My family—all ten of us!

Read all the books
about **Mallory**
in the Baby-sitters Club series
by Ann M. Martin

Look for #93

MARY ANNE AND THE MEMORY GARDEN

"Did you listen to the radio this morning?" Stacey asked.

"No," I said, trying to fluff my hair, which was still damp from the shower. "I overslept, and then Sharon was rehearsing her speech for a big presentation at work. What happened?"

"I guess there was a car accident out by the mall last night," Stacey replied. "But I only caught the tail end of the report. I didn't hear any details."

Mallory pointed to Claudia, who was waiting for us at the next corner. "Maybe Claud heard. She always listens to the radio."

I grinned. "Yeah, in hopes that school will be canceled due to snow, or rain, or — "

"Or a heat wave," Logan added, coming up beside me.

"How long have you been there?" I asked in surprise. "I didn't even hear you."

"That's because there's shampoo in your ear," Logan said, swiping at a patch of bubbles that had dried on my cheek.

I could feel myself blush down to the roots of my hair. "I was running late," I confessed. "I must not have rinsed completely."

Normally Logan would have cracked a joke at my response, but by that time we'd reached Claudia, and the look on her face stopped him.

"Did you hear?" she asked. "There was a terrible accident on the freeway just outside of town. One person was killed. A thirteen-year-old from Stoneybrook."

We all gasped.

"Did they give the name?" I whispered, afraid to hear the answer.

THE BABY-SITTERS CLUB®

Collect 'em all!

100 (and more)
Reasons to Stay Friends Forever!

❑ MG43388-1	#1	Kristy's Great Idea	$3.50
❑ MG43387-3	#10	Logan Likes Mary Anne!	$3.99
❑ MG43717-8	#15	Little Miss Stoneybrook...and Dawn	$3.50
❑ MG43722-4	#20	Kristy and the Walking Disaster	$3.50
❑ MG43347-4	#25	Mary Anne and the Search for Tigger	$3.50
❑ MG42498-X	#30	Mary Anne and the Great Romance	$3.50
❑ MG42508-0	#35	Stacey and the Mystery of Stoneybrook	$3.50
❑ MG44082-9	#40	Claudia and the Middle School Mystery	$3.25
❑ MG43574-4	#45	Kristy and the Baby Parade	$3.50
❑ MG44969-9	#50	Dawn's Big Date	$3.50
❑ MG44968-0	#51	Stacey's Ex-Best Friend	$3.50
❑ MG44966-4	#52	Mary Anne + 2 Many Babies	$3.50
❑ MG44967-2	#53	Kristy for President	$3.25
❑ MG44965-6	#54	Mallory and the Dream Horse	$3.25
❑ MG44964-8	#55	Jessi's Gold Medal	$3.25
❑ MG45657-1	#56	Keep Out, Claudia!	$3.50
❑ MG45658-X	#57	Dawn Saves the Planet	$3.50
❑ MG45659-8	#58	Stacey's Choice	$3.50
❑ MG45660-1	#59	Mallory Hates Boys (and Gym)	$3.50
❑ MG45662-8	#60	Mary Anne's Makeover	$3.50
❑ MG45663-6	#61	Jessi and the Awful Secret	$3.50
❑ MG45664-4	#62	Kristy and the Worst Kid Ever	$3.50
❑ MG45665-2	#63	Claudia's Special Friend	$3.50
❑ MG45666-0	#64	Dawn's Family Feud	$3.50
❑ MG45667-9	#65	Stacey's Big Crush	$3.50
❑ MG47004-3	#66	Maid Mary Anne	$3.50
❑ MG47005-1	#67	Dawn's Big Move	$3.50
❑ MG47006-X	#68	Jessi and the Bad Baby-sitter	$3.50
❑ MG47007-8	#69	Get Well Soon, Mallory!	$3.50
❑ MG47008-6	#70	Stacey and the Cheerleaders	$3.50
❑ MG47009-4	#71	Claudia and the Perfect Boy	$3.99
❑ MG47010-8	#72	Dawn and the We Love Kids Club	$3.99
❑ MG47011-6	#73	Mary Anne and Miss Priss	$3.99
❑ MG47012-4	#74	Kristy and the Copycat	$3.99
❑ MG47013-2	#75	Jessi's Horrible Prank	$3.50
❑ MG47014-0	#76	Stacey's Lie	$3.50
❑ MG48221-1	#77	Dawn and Whitney, Friends Forever	$3.99
❑ MG48222-X	#78	Claudia and Crazy Peaches	$3.50
❑ MG48223-8	#79	Mary Anne Breaks the Rules	$3.50
❑ MG48224-6	#80	Mallory Pike, #1 Fan	$3.99

More titles... ➤

The Baby-sitters Club titles continued...

☐ MG48225-4	#81	**Kristy and Mr. Mom**	**$3.50**
☐ MG48226-2	#82	**Jessi and the Troublemaker**	**$3.99**
☐ MG48235-1	#83	**Stacey vs. the BSC**	**$3.50**
☐ MG48228-9	#84	**Dawn and the School Spirit War**	**$3.50**
☐ MG48236-X	#85	**Claudi Kishi, Live from WSTO**	**$3.50**
☐ MG48227-0	#86	**Mary Anne and Camp BSC**	**$3.50**
☐ MG48237-8	#87	**Stacey and the Bad Girls**	**$3.50**
☐ MG22872-2	#88	**Farewell, Dawn**	**$3.50**
☐ MG22873-0	#89	**Kristy and the Dirty Diapers**	**$3.50**
☐ MG22874-9	#90	**Welcome to the BSC, Abby**	**$3.50**
☐ MG22875-1	#91	**Claudia and the First Thanksgiving**	**$3.50**
☐ MG22876-5	#92	**Mallory's Christmas Wish**	**$3.50**
☐ MG22877-3	#93	**Mary Anne and the Memory Garden**	**$3.99**
☐ MG22878-1	#94	**Stacey McGill, Super Sitter**	**$3.99**
☐ MG22879-X	#95	**Kristy + Bart = ?**	**$3.99**
☐ MG22880-3	#96	**Abby's Lucky Thirteen**	**$3.99**
☐ MG22881-1	#97	**Claudia and the World's Cutest Baby**	**$3.99**
☐ MG22882-X	#98	**Dawn and Too Many Baby-sitters**	**$3.99**
☐ MG69205-4	#99	**Stacey's Broken Heart**	**$3.99**
☐ MG69206-2	#100	**Kristy's Worst Idea**	**$3.99**
☐ MG45575-3		**Logan's Story Special Edition Readers' Request**	**$3.25**
☐ MG47118-X		**Logan Bruno, Boy Baby-sitter**	
		Special Edition Readers' Request	**$3.50**
☐ MG47756-0		**Shannon's Story Special Edition**	**$3.50**
☐ MG47686-6		**The Baby-sitters Club Guide to Baby-sitting**	**$3.25**
☐ MG47314-X		**The Baby-sitters Club Trivia and Puzzle Fun Book**	**$2.50**
☐ MG48400-1		**BSC Portrait Collection: Claudia's Book**	**$3.50**
☐ MG22864-1		**BSC Portrait Collection: Dawn's Book**	**$3.50**
☐ MG69181-3		**BSC Portrait Collection: Kristy's Book**	**$3.99**
☐ MG22865-X		**BSC Portrait Collection: Mary Anne's Book**	**$3.99**
☐ MG48399-4		**BSC Portrait Collection: Stacey's Book**	**$3.50**
☐ MG92713-2		**The Complete Guide to the Baby-sitters Club**	**$4.95**
☐ MG47151-1		**The Baby-sitters Club Chain Letter**	**$14.95**
☐ MG48295-5		**The Baby-sitters Club Secret Santa**	**$14.95**
☐ MG45074-3		**The Baby-sitters Club Notebook**	**$2.50**
☐ MG44783-1		**The Baby-sitters Club Postcard Book**	**$4.95**

Available wherever you buy books...or use this order form.
Scholastic Inc., P.O. Box 7502, 2931 E. McCarty Street, Jefferson City, MO 65102

Please send me the books I have checked above. I am enclosing $_____
(please add $2.00 to cover shipping and handling). Send check or money order—
no cash or C.O.D.s please.

Name_____ Birthdate_____

Address _____

City_____ State/Zip _____

Please allow four to six weeks for delivery. Offer good in the U.S. only. Sorry,
mail orders are not available to residents of Canada. Prices subject to change.

BSC596

Now THE BABY·SITTERS CLUB®

is a Video Club too!

THE BABY-SITTERS CLUB®

by Ann M. Martin

Meet the best friends you'll ever have!

Have you heard? The BSC has a new look — and more great stuff than ever before. An all-new scrapbook for each book's narrator! A letter from Ann M. Martin! Fill-in pages to personalize your copy! Order today!

☐ BBD22473-5	#1	**Kristy's Great Idea**	$3.50
☐ BBD22763-7	#2	**Claudia and the Phantom Phone Calls**	$3.99
☐ BBD25158-9	#3	**The Truth About Stacey**	$3.99
☐ BBD25159-7	#4	**Mary Anne Saves the Day**	$3.50
☐ BBD25160-0	#5	**Dawn and the Impossible Three**	$3.50
☐ BBD25161-9	#6	**Kristy's Big Day**	$3.50
☐ BBD25162-7	#7	**Claudia and Mean Janine**	$3.50
☐ BBD25163-5	#8	**Boy Crazy Stacey**	$3.50
☐ BBD25164-3	#9	**The Ghost at Dawn's House**	$3.99
☐ BBD25165-1	#10	**Logan Likes Mary Anne!**	$3.99
☐ BBD25166-X	#11	**Kristy and the Snobs**	$3.99
☐ BBD25167-8	#12	**Claudia and the New Girl**	$3.99
☐ BBD25168-6	#13	**Good-bye Stacey, Good-bye**	$3.99
☐ BBD25169-4	#14	**Hello, Mallory**	$3.99
☐ BBD25169-4	#15	**Little Miss Stoneybrook...and Dawn**	$3.99
☐ BBD60410-4	#16	**Jessi's Secret Language**	$3.99
☐ BBD60428-7	#17	**Mary Anne's Bad Luck Mystery**	$3.99

Available wherever you buy books, or use this order form.

THE BABY-SITTERS CLUB®

by Ann M. Martin

Collect and read these exciting BSC Super Specials, Mysteries, and Super Mysteries along with your favorite Baby-sitters Club books!

BSC Super Specials

❏ BBK44240-6	Baby-sitters on Board! Super Special #1	$3.95
❏ BBK44239-2	Baby-sitters' Summer Vacation Super Special #2	$3.95
❏ BBK43973-1	Baby-sitters' Winter Vacation Super Special #3	$3.95
❏ BBK42493-9	Baby-sitters' Island Adventure Super Special #4	$3.95
❏ BBK43575-2	California Girls! Super Special #5	$3.95
❏ BBK43576-0	New York, New York! Super Special #6	$4.50
❏ BBK44963-X	Snowbound! Super Special #7	$3.95
❏ BBK44962-X	Baby-sitters at Shadow Lake Super Special #8	$3.95
❏ BBK45661-X	Starring The Baby-sitters Club! Super Special #9	$3.95
❏ BBK45674-1	Sea City, Here We Come! Super Special #10	$3.95
❏ BBK47015-9	The Baby-sitters Remember Super Special #11	$3.95
❏ BBK48308-0	Here Come the Bridesmaids! Super Special #12	$3.95
❏ BBK22883-8	Aloha, Baby-sitters! Super Special #13	$4.50

BSC Mysteries

❏ BAI44084-5	#1 Stacey and the Missing Ring	$3.50
❏ BAI44085-3	#2 Beware Dawn!	$3.50
❏ BAI44799-8	#3 Mallory and the Ghost Cat	$3.50
❏ BAI44800-5	#4 Kristy and the Missing Child	$3.50
❏ BAI44801-3	#5 Mary Anne and the Secret in the Attic	$3.50
❏ BAI44961-3	#6 The Mystery at Claudia's House	$3.50
❏ BAI44960-5	#7 Dawn and the Disappearing Dogs	$3.50
❏ BAI44959-1	#8 Jessi and the Jewel Thieves	$3.50
❏ BAI44958-3	#9 Kristy and the Haunted Mansion	$3.50
❏ BAI45696-2	#10 Stacey and the Mystery Money	$3.50

More titles ➡

The Baby-sitters Club books continued...

❑ BAI47049-3	#11 Claudia and the Mystery at the Museum	$3.50
❑ BAI47050-7	#12 Dawn and the Surfer Ghost	$3.50
❑ BAI47051-5	#13 Mary Anne and the Library Mystery	$3.50
❑ BAI47052-3	#14 Stacey and the Mystery at the Mall	$3.50
❑ BAI47053-1	#15 Kristy and the Vampires	$3.50
❑ BAI47054-X	#16 Claudia and the Clue in the Photograph	$3.99
❑ BAI48232-7	#17 Dawn and the Halloween Mystery	$3.50
❑ BAI48233-5	#18 Stacey and the Mystery at the Empty House	$3.50
❑ BAI48234-3	#19 Kristy and the Missing Fortune	$3.50
❑ BAI48309-9	#20 Mary Anne and the Zoo Mystery	$3.50
❑ BAI48310-2	#21 Claudia and the Recipe for Danger	$3.50
❑ BAI22866-8	#22 Stacey and the Haunted Masquerade	$3.50
❑ BAI22867-6	#23 Abby and the Secret Society	$3.99
❑ BAI22868-4	#24 Mary Anne and the Silent Witness	$3.99
❑ BAI22869-2	#25 Kristy and the Middle School Vandal	$3.99
❑ BAI22870-6	#26 Dawn Schafer, Undercover Baby-sitter	$3.99

BSC Super Mysteries

❑ BAI48311-0	The Baby-sitters' Haunted House Super Mystery #1	$3.99
❑ BAI22871-4	Baby-sitters Beware Super Mystery #2	$3.99
❑ BAI69180-5	Baby-sitters' Fright Night Super Mystery #3	$4.50

Available wherever you buy books...or use this order form.

Scholastic Inc., P.O. Box 7502, 2931 East McCarty Street, Jefferson City, MO 65102-7502

Please send me the books I have checked above. I am enclosing $ _____
(please add $2.00 to cover shipping and handling). Send check or money order
— no cash or C.O.D.s please.

Name_____Birthdate_____

Address _____

City_____State/Zip_____

Please allow four to six weeks for delivery. Offer good in the U.S. only. Sorry, mail orders are not available to residents of Canada. Prices subject to change.

BSCM496